Maura's Dance with Uncle Sam

Michael G. Casey

ISBN 978-1-9160264-1-4

First edition, 2019

Published by Azimuth Publishing
Dublin, Ireland

Cover image of Capitol Building: by John Brighenti via
Flickr; the image has been altered.

Layout, cover design by iCulture

Please visit michaelgcasey.com

ABOUT THIS BOOK

Maura, a shy Englishwoman, works for her dentist husband, Harold, who tries to restrict her many outside interests. To his chagrin, Maura appears on a major TV Quiz show. She wins a prize to visit the US and attend a Celebrity New Year's Eve Ball in Washington DC.

Patrick, a Frenchman, embarks on a dangerous geo-political mission. He kidnaps Harold and poses as Maura's husband. She has no option but to travel with him to the US, where they meet with celebrities, other prize-winners, and senior political figures. She is racked by guilt, but her worries shift as she realises that Patrick is more a misguided idealist than a terrorist. She can't help being drawn towards him. Maura begins to fear for her life – and his.

The Washington Ball approaches. Tight security is coordinated by a shrewd and ambitious FBI agent with support from Homeland Security. Maura tries desperately to persuade Patrick to abort his mission.

Maura grows in adversity, becomes stronger and more questioning. Even in captivity, Harold is the same old fogey. Then after all seems lost, Maura makes a remarkable discovery that will change everything…

"Against a backdrop of Washington covert dealing and heartless calculation, two figures find their truer selves. Patrick's idealism battles with human desire. As the plot develops, carefully and unpredictably, we see Maura unfold too, as stronger and more complex than she ever imagined. In a deft storyline told as though in a single breath, the inevitable crisis is a long-delayed reckoning."

—Peter FitzGerald

BOOKS PREVIOUSLY PUBLISHED
BY MICHAEL G. CASEY

Come Home, Robbie, a novel, published by The O'Brien Press, 1990

> "…page-turning urgency … spine-tingling compulsion … the sheer quality of the writing lends the story some of the stature of heroic tragedy."
> —The Education Times

Treadmill, an award-winning Chapbook of short stories, published by Tipperary Arts Centre and Start Magazine, 2008

> "…Casey brings to life vivid characters who captivate, amuse and engage … (He) has a wry observation and quick wit."
> —Mike McCormack

Ireland's Malaise: The Troubled Personality of the Irish Economy, published by The Liffey Press, 2010

> "…(Casey) shows the same Confucian wisdom as his hero, T.K. Whitaker in his brilliant new book."

—Eoghan Harris, The Sunday Independent

The Visit, a novel, published by The Anaphora Press, 2011

> "…a small Irish town deals with a major event … an interesting addition to the genre … clear-eyed … vivid description…"
> —Denis Fahey, Historian

> "…a lovely clear prose style … some great characters and beautifully crafted vignettes."
> —Stella Kane, Quartet Books Ltd

Broken Circle, a collection of poetry, due to be published by Salmon Press in Spring 2019

> "…very powerful, intelligent poems made their presence known immediately … (Casey) uses casuistry and persuasiveness to rival Robert Browning's dramatic Monologues…"
> —Derek Selen

Michael G. Casey's most recent novels, *Smudged Mascara* and *The Killing of Ros Grenham*, from Azimuth Publishing, are available in Kindle and print versions through Amazon.

DEDICATION

For: Saoirse, Orlagh, Cian, Isabella and Darren.

CHAPTER 1

IT WAS JUST after midday in the town of St. Meurat some thirty kilometres south-east of Poitiers. Patrick Delaborde had a word with Paul, who sat in the passenger seat of the black Toyota Avensis. Then he got out of the car and walked towards the main intersection of the town which featured an old ornate drinking trough for horses.

The sun beat down on him and more than once he tilted back the peak of the gendarme's hat and passed a hand across his brow. At the south side of the intersection where the narrow Rue de Copains began, he stopped, dialled the number of the adjacent bank on his phone, and asked to speak to the manager. Without any attempt to disguise his voice he told him there was a bomb in the bank which would detonate in fifteen minutes.

He waited while the manager went through the gamut of shock and incredulity.

"This is not a hoax. You're wasting time. You must evacuate the staff now. Immediately."

"But … but how do I know … Why should I believe…?" The manager blustered but his voice had risen to a pitch of near hysteria.

"This call is being recorded," Patrick interrupted. "If people die it will be known that you bungled. You have less than fourteen minutes." He ended the call, put the phone in the top pocket of his uniform and started to walk down the Rue de Copains.

Although he knew it couldn't fail – no one could afford not to take a bomb threat seriously – he was nevertheless relieved to see in the distance the staff of the bank begin to spill out onto the street. Under the excitable guidance of the manager they walked hurriedly and in disarray to their muster point which happened to be outside a pâtisserie less than two hundred metres from where he stood. He observed the manager doing a head count of his staff in a very flustered manner.

Patrick adjusted the tunic of his heavy serge uniform and walked towards them, feeling the sweat gather in his armpits.

As expected, the manager rushed towards him and breathlessly told him about the bomb threat.

"Do something, officer. Please … You must…"

"How long since the call?" Patrick demanded.

"What?"

"Minutes … How many minutes since the phone call?"

"Four or five … maybe."

"That leaves up to ten … Are all the staff out?"

"Yes." Obsessively, the manager started to count them again. It was difficult since they kept moving about excitedly.

"It may be a hoax," Patrick said. "But I must check." He added that he would phone the bomb squad from inside the bank. He asked for the keys and codes which the manager promptly provided.

"Please hurry," he said in a voice that was close to breaking.

Patrick ran towards the bank.

The chief cashier moved to the manager's side to lend him moral support. They had soldiered together for over twenty years – going from ledgers to laptops – but had never encountered anything quite like this.

"I suppose it had to happen sooner or later," she said comfortingly. "The way things are nowadays. What with terrorism and everything else."

The manager mumbled his agreement with little grace. "Ever since the financial collapse, bankers get no respect. None whatsoever."

Inside the bank, Patrick opened his tunic and pulled out a silk carry-all which had been folded to the size of a paperback book. He shook it out and worked feverishly. The intelligence had been good. The tellers' drawers were full in anticipation of the town's pay-day. He made a rough approximation of the amounts as he emptied the drawers into the bag. He also managed to empty the ATM machine – a nice bonus. It was a pity about the vaults. He had neither the time nor the expertise. Still, enough was enough. He took one last look around, zipped up the bag and went out through the rear exit. He passed quickly through a cobbled courtyard flanked by old coach-houses, reached the alley and got into the back of the waiting Toyota. Paul turned to him, with an anxious look on his face, "OK?"

"Yes." Patrick was still tense and didn't feel much like talking. He removed the hat and false moustache. "We have enough cash here I think." He and Paul would verify that later when they planned the next, crucial, phase of their strategy: the assassination of Lawrence T. Dwyer, who headed up one of the largest and most politically connected arms manufacturing companies in the US.

The driver nosed the car out of the alley and headed south along a minor road, keeping carefully to the speed limit. Paul studied a map which rested on his knee.

"Planning pays. It worked like a charm." Paul laughed softly. "That's a good omen, Patrick."

"I hope so. It's only beginning." There were so many uncertainties, he thought, that couldn't be planned for in advance, especially the means of gaining access to the exclusive event that was to be hosted by Lawrence T. Dwyer in Washington D.C. He could only guess at what the security would be like. They had discussed a number of possibilities, the least flawed of which involved London as a starting point.

"Any doubts?" Paul turned to look at him.

"No." Patrick had many doubts about logistics but none about the objective, none at all.

"We can pick up the autoroute at Poitiers, then head for Tours and Chartres. Keep west of Paris," Paul told the driver who nodded. "By my reckoning we'll make the Channel Tunnel by 17.30 at the latest.

A good half hour later the bank manager conferred nervously with his chief cashier. He called the police who in turn contacted the bomb disposal unit. No report had been received by them.

The manager felt faint. And fainter still when he surveyed the ransacked drawers and cash machines of his bank. He had hoped to retire with a clean record. Now he realized he had fallen at the last fence, and been duped in the worst possible way. He anticipated the sympathetic clucking of his wife that evening when the news came on, and dreaded it.

CHAPTER 2

HAROLD CROWTHER SAT in his recliner reading those columns of the Financial Times that he'd not had time to read during his busy day. The pair of half-glasses that perched on the bony bridge of his nose gave him a professorial look. Managing his financial portfolio relaxed him after a hard day drilling teeth and sweating over a hot autoclave. The day he mastered options trading, he hummed all the way home on the train. Of course, he never proffered financial advice to friends or neighbours; that would be courting disaster. Besides, he preferred to keep his financial affairs private. His own adviser had convinced him that, following the triple-dip recession of the West, the market was bound to recover if not indeed find itself in a bullish feeding frenzy. That opinion had served him well. Most of the money created by quantitative easing had gone into equities, so the last two years had been exceptionally good ones, and he had made a bundle. Part of his satisfaction came from keeping the good news entirely to himself.

His wife Maura was in the small dining room ostensibly watching TV, but paying more attention to a Wikipedia page on General Knowledge which she had opened on her laptop. In her mid-thirties, she was considerably younger than Harold and her startling blue eyes made her seem vivacious. She could see Harold through the open door and was quite happy to leave him to his 'investments'.

She still worked as his receptionist / hygienist and had spent more years than she cared to remember mixing amalgams and suctioning out of innumerable mouths the detritus of Harold's often imprecise drilling. They had spent long hours together as he was building up his practice – 'drilling for oil' he called it. She came to understand his instructions, delivered in a ritual mumble through his hygiene mask, and they developed a good rapport. Once when he was sued by a woman patient – an occlusal reconstruction job – on the grounds that the different amalgams caused electric shocks in her mouth, Maura stood by him and persuaded the patient to settle out of court for a modest amount. He came to depend on her as an office manager; she did the books, and generally ran the practice. She and Harold became close and drifted into marriage as if it were the logical next step in a sequence. She didn't regret it and had learned to cope with his little quirks and vanities.

After about three years of marriage she decided unilaterally to go off the pill. When Harold found out he was furious. He wasn't ready for children and, in his opinion, she should have consulted him. When, sometime later, they did try to start a family, nothing happened. Maura was struck by the irony but Harold was annoyed and assumed it was her fault. She had medical tests which by deduction indicated that the problem lay with Harold, but every time she broached the subject he either laughed at her or went into a sulk. He refused doggedly to go for tests. Sometimes she wanted to shake him. But not this evening. There was something else on her mind.

One of her hobbies, apart from bridge, was quiz competitions and she had built up a good store of general knowledge, aided by the internet and an excellent memory. She had done well in local pub quizzes, usually organised for charitable purposes, and, about a month earlier, had conceived the notion of going on a TV quiz show. Harold was singularly unimpressed.

"It would be too public," he'd said. "You shouldn't do it." In fact, this particular quiz show had received saturation publicity not just by the TV channel concerned but also by the sponsors who bought space in social media, the broadsheets and the tabloids.

"Why not?" Although she knew how stuffy he could be, the strength of his reaction came as something of a surprise. "There's nothing to be ashamed of. All right, I mightn't win but I'm not going to disgrace myself."

"There are standards…" he insisted. "We live here in Hertfordshire, in a small community. In my…our profession appearances are important. It's a question of credibility … of appropriate behaviour and decorum. Charity functions are one thing but this is different. It's a … a glitzy show. No, it's not on."

"Harold, I'm not going to dance on table tops…"

"Take my advice and forget about it, Maura. Even if you win, you lose."

"What does that mean?" She pushed her plate away from her.

"Imagine accepting such a tawdry prize from our American cousins! Who do they think they are, distributing largesse to Britons and Europeans?" He went back to his Sunday pot-roast, wearing a frown that took a while to dissolve.

But Maura didn't forget about it. In fact she'd already been accepted as a contestant after an audition in which she'd forced herself to be more exuberant than usual. The top prize appealed greatly to her: tickets for two to New York and Washington for Christmas and the New Year, including invitations to a very swish ball. This prize had been on offer every year for the past decade; she wasn't sure why. Maybe America decided to go on a charm offensive for reasons best known to itself. She didn't really care. But this year, she wanted to be there, though not entirely sure why. Maura wanted to win that prize more than anything else, and Harold's fastidious hang-ups weren't going to stop her having a go. As one of four contestants she stood a reasonable chance and had been mugging up her general knowledge ever since the audition. She had bought or borrowed the standard texts and supplemented these with the internet. Whenever there was some downtime in the dental practice, she would hide away in the waiting room and study her quiz materials.

She looked at the clock in the dining room with mounting excitement. It was time to go to the TV studios. With Harold still immersed in the Financial Times, leaving the house would not present insuperable difficulties; explaining things later on would, however, be another day's work, but she couldn't concern herself with that now. She checked her handbag and as she passed the open door into the lounge, said casually, "I'm going out for a while, Dear."

"Where?" He didn't look up from the paper.

"Bridge." It wasn't her bridge night but he didn't register that. Nor did he notice her new hair-do. He just gave his usual sniff as if she were continuing to live the high life at his expense.

She drove herself in the Ford Fiesta to the station and got the train into London. As the train hurtled between stations she had a sense of inevitability that was strangely calming. The die was cast. During the short cab ride to the studios, however, her nerves began to work on her and she knew that the real contest would be fought out inside herself.

A couple of hours before Maura had left her home in Hertingfordbury three men got into a Toyota outside a run-down guest house in Kilburn and drove towards the West End.

"This really is a long shot," Patrick said, having expressed a similar sentiment in different ways several times over.

"Yes," Paul agreed. "But if it works it could be perfect. If it doesn't, we go back to the drawing board. The cash gives us options."

"Maybe we could have chosen another European city as the starting point?"

"London is the least worst option," Paul said. "The organization is still below the radar there. Also, we may benefit from the so-called special relationship between the UK and US."

"Let's hope so."

At a set of traffic lights Patrick noticed a passenger in an adjacent car. Although the physical resemblance was slight, there was something about him which reminded him of his brother. Similar instances had occurred frequently in Paris in the aftermath of the tragedy. He wondered if the memory would fade in time, if the pain would ease. He doubted it. His brother's death had been violent in the extreme, and it had changed Patrick's life forever.

"I probably won't be able to park at the

studios," the driver said.

"That's OK," Paul told him. "You can just drop us off and drive around for as long as it takes. We'll keep in touch on the phones."

He and Patrick joined the queue outside the studios. They had already checked that admission would be on a first-come basis. There were only about a dozen people ahead of them so there was no difficulty about getting in. They sat in the tiered seats with the rest of the studio audience, feeling ill at ease. The show was not due to start for another thirty-five minutes.

———

A receptionist led Maura into a hospitality room where she met the other three contestants. They chatted in desultory fashion, each trying to figure out how tough the opposition was going to be. One man looked awfully studious and her heart sank. After a brief pitstop in the make-up department the contestants were shepherded to the studio and introduced to Reg Davis, the emcee. Maura was struck by his easy charm and couldn't help noticing the very heavy make-up beneath his eyes. Harold no doubt would have questioned his sexual orientation, as he was wont to do about most people in showbiz.

"The prog is being recorded," Reg

explained to them, "so we can edit out any bloopers. No one is going to be embarrassed. It's not that kind of show. OK? OK, Maura?"

"Yes." She wondered why he'd singled her out for reassurance. Were her nerves showing? Did he see her as the weak link, the one most likely to throw a wobbly? The other woman certainly seemed calm and self-contained.

Harold was bound to hear about her appearance even if she managed to divert him from seeing the actual broadcast. Still, if by some stroke of luck she managed to win and presented him with his airline tickets, he would surely swallow his pride. Better to put thoughts of winning out of her mind …

As if on cue Reg said, "The important thing is to have fun. It's a game, nothing more. And don't be afraid to let your feelings show." It often intrigued him how the losers hardly ever seemed disappointed, on screen at least. Maybe they felt suicidal afterwards but while on camera they appeared to be genuinely unconcerned. Part of the magic of the medium, he supposed. Just as well for him. Nothing would be worse than having to commiserate with a poor loser. He continued to smile at his four contestants, briefed them on the format and reminded them of the rules.

He cupped his ear piece to listen to the invisible producer. "OK everybody, show-time. Just ignore the cameras and the audience. And good luck." He led them on to the set which seemed remarkably makeshift and tinselly to Maura. She was dazzled by the powerful Kleig lights but, mercifully, they prevented her from seeing the audience – apart from the few blurred faces in the front row. She sat weakly at her individual dais; it was like facing a firing squad. Her name was on the front of the dais and the dreaded buzzer sat on top of it.

Reg cracked a few jokes with the studio audience and told them of the star prize that was on offer – the 'annual chance to dance with Uncle Sam'. "Be generous with your applause," he added. "It's not easy for the contestants. Give them encouragement."

The studio manager gave him the half-minute sign; the cameramen were in place.

"Lights up ... and clear!" someone announced. Reg turned to one of the cameras and went into his introductory spiel. He seemed to come even more alive and grew visibly excited when he described the high stakes they were playing for, which came courtesy of a US television network owned by Lawrence T. Dwyer.

Maura had heard the name; she was sure that Harold invested in his companies. Reg then introduced the contestants individually, chatting to them about their jobs and hobbies. They weren't just raw material for the show, he seemed to be saying, but real people. When he came to Maura she felt that her responses were leaden, dredged up. A strange sensation came over her. She wanted to rise to the occasion – to help make it a successful show – more than she wanted to win. It was crazy. She would have to force herself to concentrate on the main chance.

The first round was about music, middle-brow for the most part. The studious-looking man, Michael, hit the deck running. Maura felt she knew as many of the answers as he did but he beat her to the buzzer every time. Whenever she did hit the damn thing it made no sound because his buzzer had cancelled it. Without some kind of positive reinforcement she began to panic and in an odd way that helped because it made her dive in a fraction of a second before she was sure of the answer. Towards the end of the round she answered two Gilbert and Sullivan questions correctly even though Reg had to hurry her. He complimented her when she broke her duck, and that helped her confidence a little. Still, at the end of that round Michael had built up a commanding lead and the other two had also done better than she had.

From that point on she knew she had nothing to lose. She threw caution to the winds and went for the buzzer whenever she had the faintest inkling of an answer. She was in a lather of concentration, was only vaguely aware of the excited applause of the audience and had no real sense that she had actually taken a slight lead.

The pause for the commercial break came and went. She resented the break, indeed was afraid of it, and was unable to join in any of the chit-chat. She did, however, appreciate a drink of ice-cold water and the ministrations of the make-up girl who powder-puffed her glistening forehead.

In the penultimate round of 'Pick a Category' Michael drew level again and from then on it was nip and tuck. The other two had dropped out of contention. Reg's deliberate – and unnecessary – hyping of the tension passed her by. His frequent references to the cash already accumulated didn't register with her, nor the manic tone of voice he adopted when putting the questions. She heard only the words. Hitting the buzzer had become a dangerous reflex. She miscued a number of times and it cost her, but she couldn't hold off. One step back, two forward. A gambler's desperate urge had taken her over. Where it might ultimately have led would never be known because a strange gong-like sound, dimly heard by Maura, ended the round.

"Wow, Maura, that was absolutely fantastic," Reg enthused. "Ladies and gentlemen…" He didn't have to exhort the audience; they applauded and cheered spontaneously.

"My god," she thought, "I've done it." Her legs went weak and she had to use the dais for support. But she hadn't done it, not yet. She'd merely qualified for the final question.

"Maura, you've already won twelve

thousand, six hundred pounds," Reg announced. "Now would you please join me for the star prize question."

She looked vacantly at his extended hand and did a double-take. Christ, another hurdle, the last and most important one. Would her luck hold for just one more question? Trance-like she watched a computer screen generate different categories. When the flickering images stopped Reg said in hushed tones, "Geography, Maura. OK? One question for the star prize." He riffled through a pack of gold-edged cards and selected one, holding it close to his chest. "You have twenty seconds to answer. You know the rules. We have to apply them strictly." He had become as grave and unctuous as an undertaker.

"Get on with it, you dope," she thought with a sudden spurt of anger. This was demeaning. Had Harold been right all along? Reg helped her to her mark and looked closely into her eyes. The studio seemed the quietest place on earth. She knew that one of those sinister cameras had zoomed in on her, showing every pore in her face.

"Now, Maura," Reg began slowly and with an expression of anguished concern, "for the trip of a lifetime … organised by our American cousins," He glanced again at the card and started to enunciate with infinite care and gravity, "can you tell me … the name … of the capital … of Mongolia? Your time starts now!"

He stepped back slightly to emphasise that this was her moment; she was on her own.

Instinctively, her hand went for an imaginary buzzer. But it was a bluff. She didn't know the answer. Oh god, to fall at the last fence. Those bastards. This was what they wanted. Humiliation … good TV. The capital of Mongolia. Did it really matter? She had never seen the word written down. That was certain. Then something stirred. What…?

"Have to hurry you, Maura," Reg said in a gentle concerned whisper. His eyes were sad. Maybe he did want her to win. What stirred in her mind was a sound that seemed to chime with the sound of Mongolia. It came from deep inside and emerged from her throat in a halting croak, "U-u-long Ba-a-ter."

"I didn't quite … could you repeat…?" Was Reg encouraging her or setting her up for the final humiliation? In for a penny … "Ulong Bater," she repeated with as much conviction as she could muster, and then some. She threw the sounds at his feet.

The second of silence was the longest she'd ever endured.

"Ulaanbaater," Reg said carefully, hesitating over each syllable as if he wanted to check that the sounds were reasonably close to those she had uttered. "Yes. Correct!" The audience exploded. All the computerised strobes and klaxons of the studio burst into action. The next thing Maura knew was that she was in his arms being lifted off her feet. The other contestants rushed to congratulate her. Tears came to her eyes. In a sobbing daze she accepted the airline tickets, invitation cards and cash which were doled out by the sympathetically ecstatic quizmaster.

The mood of celebration lasted until she left the hospitality room and then, at some stage on the train home, changed into a sour aftertaste. She'd won; no-one could deny that. She'd achieved what she'd set her heart on, but at what cost? She recoiled from that gambler's high that had given her an unsettling insight into herself. She felt drained and exploited, and she still had to face Harold and the neighbours. There was a mordant sense of having exposed some vain and grasping part of her nature. The feeling of anti-climax was probably not unlike post-partum depression. She despised herself for having cried – like the winner of some goddam beauty contest. And she hadn't got the final answer right, not really. She didn't have a clue how to spell it or even if it was one word or two. She had just summoned up a credible sound, parrot-fashion. While the residents of Mongolia might forgive her, she doubted if Harold and the cognoscenti in Hertfordshire would.

She brought her handbag to her lap and went through the invitations, tours, receptions and concerts in New York and Washington, culminating in the New Year's Eve Ball. She was sure to rally over the coming days but tonight had to be coped with somehow. Or maybe she wouldn't rally. Maybe she was a silly woman, sliding into middle age, her bio-clock running down, hoping for a final fling, a New Year's Eve to beat all others. Why did it mean so much to her anyway? Her grandmother – whom she adored – was born on New Year's Day 1920 and had always spoken of America as the hope for the future, even for the human species. But her grandmother had also believed in magic, old wives' tales and fertility rites. Men, she claimed, could not understand these things and were far too practical for their own good.

She crept into bed that night beside the sleeping form of Harold as if she'd just come from the arms of a lover – fat chance.

After the show when Maura had left the studios, the two men followed her on foot to the nearest tube station. They boarded the same carriage of the train and sat in silence for the duration of the journey.

When she got out at her stop and walked towards the car park they realised with some alarm that she was going to drive the rest of the way. They managed to get one of the few taxis outside the station in the nick of time. Paul told the taxi driver that he wasn't sure of the address he wanted but that he knew the route and would direct him. He couldn't take the risk of telling the cabbie to follow the Ford Fiesta in case he was a local man, possibly even a friend of Maura's.

One advantage of the narrow roads was that the taxi could not pass out the Fiesta. In the middle of Hertingfordbury Maura turned into the little driveway of her nominally detached house, switched off the engine and got out.

As they drove by Paul and Patrick made mental notes of the house. They exchanged glances. Patrick nodded; he could find the house again.

They drove on to the next village, called at an unlit house from which there was no response. Paul pretended that there must have been a glitch in communications. They asked the cabbie to drop them back to the station.

When they returned to the guest house in Kilburn it was about 1.00 a.m. They stayed up for another couple of hours talking in low tones, building on what they'd established so far. It was a shaky foundation and the woman who won the prize seemed emotional and unreliable, but it was probably the best opportunity they were going to get. Paul then made a call to Paris.

CHAPTER 3

FROM THE BREAKFAST room Lawrence T. Dwyer could see occasionally – when the air quality permitted – the bay area, the Golden Gate Bridge and sometimes Alcatraz. This morning the air was heavy and sulphur-laden. He was a well-built man in his early forties, his fair hair just beginning to turn grey at the ends of his well-barbered sideburns. That he was driven, if not indeed a workaholic, could be seen at a glance in the frank, alert eyes and the almost ascetic bone structure of his face.

His wife, Amanda, had gone to the Caribbean. It didn't bother him too much if she was having another affair. In dynastic – and contractual – marriages one didn't worry about that as long as any indiscretions were kept out of the public gaze. That, indeed, was the way he conducted his own liaisons. Amanda and he actually had a reasonable modus vivendi; each understood, and followed the rules. Discretion was everything.

He himself avoided publicity to a pathological degree, preferring to operate behind the scenes. Ever since 9/11 and the Iraq and Syrian wars, there was a growing awareness of a deep state which influenced many national policy decisions – an awareness that was too close for comfort. He was a producer who didn't want his name to appear in the credits.

He had inherited this attitude from his German grandfather who would not have been able to grow his business if the media had put him under the microscope as he set about upgrading German armaments, particularly the Wurfgranate 42 Spreng and the Raketenwerfer 61. Nowadays, even though the mainstream media played ball, there were many mavericks out there using social media to critique national policy at every turn. They were predators who justified everything they did on the grounds of transparency, liberal democracy and all that cant. Wikileaks was a case in point. No, he didn't want them within spitting distance, unless it was on his terms. The company's PR staff did not have an easy time.

When Lawrence took over the company he changed its name to Kaltronics and adopted his mother's maiden name. Kaltronics had produced many of the smart bombs and missiles used to devastating effect during the Gulf and Iraq Wars. In the post-nuclear era highly sophisticated 'conventional' weapons were at a premium and Kaltronics had gone from strength to strength under Lawrence's single-minded leadership. His PR people had persuaded him to cut back on laser weapons and anti-personnel mines which had been blacklisted by liberals. But they knew little about a radically new project that Lawrence had just launched; it was strictly on a need-to-know basis. He had taken their advice about buying a television network (KNYBS) partly as a front and partly as a means of moulding public opinion.

After breakfast Lawrence did a few lengths of the roof-top pool, one of his few luxuries, then showered and dressed. The presence of his security men irritated him; they were always in his peripheral vision. He tolerated them only because his Board colleagues insisted on them being there. At 8.00 a.m. exactly, one of his Vice Presidents, Bob Carraway, called to the house and joined him in a cup of coffee and planned the day's events with the aid of their electronic diaries. Bob agreed to visit Professor Lassiter at Stanford to discuss a possible solution for the guidance system of the third-generation Exocet.

"You'd better take a couple of our own eggheads with you," Lawrence suggested.

"Sure thing." Bob was not in the least offended by the implication that some of the technical stuff might be beyond him.

"I have to go to Washington to shake some trees," Lawrence said.

"In the Rose Garden, I presume?" Bob grinned.

"Not quite. But close enough. Stanley Ralston."

"Ah." Bob was impressed. Congressman Ralston was Chairman of the Committee on

American Strategic Alliances, commonly referred to as CASA, which oversaw several important Federal Agencies and had a direct line to the Pentagon and the White House.

"He owes you big time," Bob added. "Our contributions are up fifteen percent already this year, in line with your directive."

"Good. I'll probably have time to look in on the Beltway boys and see what they've been up to."

"As you know, they've changed lobbyists. You might ask them how the new guys are working out. We could do with more regular reports to HQ as well."

"Not a bad idea," Lawrence said. "We don't want them becoming an independent republic or going off the reservation."

Bob helped himself to some more coffee. "Do you think you could swing by the TV network?"

"There would be time to put down in New York," Lawrence admitted. "But, hell, that's not really my scene."

"OK. Cronin's going east next week. I'll ask him to stop off. By the way, most of the New Year's prizes have been awarded in the different countries. The reaction has been really good. The PR guys have earned their keep for once."

"Christ, I have to appear at that damn Ball, don't I?"

" 'Fraid so." Bob seemed to enjoy his

Chief's discomfiture. "You're the star attraction," he ribbed him. His attempt at humour was lost on his boss.

They discussed some other items of business then went their separate ways. Lawrence's driver brought him to the airport, where the jet was fuelled and ready. The pilot welcomed him on board.

"I'm on my own today, Frank," Lawrence told him. "You can take off as soon as you're cleared. Any problems in DC?"

"No, sir. We may have to stack for a while over Reagan Airport. But nothing worse than usual."

"Good." Lawrence buckled himself into the seat and spread his papers on the desk. He wondered if he would meet Evelyn on this trip, considered it unlikely and put the thought out of his head. He was deeply immersed in work even before they were airborne. This was quality time; he had some of his best ideas flying through limitless space.

CHAPTER 4

IT PROVED EASY enough for Maura to prevent Harold from seeing the broadcast of the quiz show, but she knew that he would hear about it sooner or later. Already some of the neighbours were buzzing with it. One of them, Barbara Woodside, fell on her at the supermarket on Saturday morning.

"Oh you lucky thing." She piled on exuberance.

"Luck had nothing to do with it," Maura replied with a laugh. She still didn't know how to cope with her own success.

"No, of course not," Barbara said hurriedly. "But imagine … that trip. God, I'd give my right arm to go. Harold must be delighted too."

Maura murmured noncommittally. Although her anti-climactic blues had lifted she was still faced with the problem of telling Harold. And time was pressing because it would be worse if he found out from another source.

Barbara continued to enthuse and Maura had to match her excitement in much the same way as she'd hammed it up on the TV show.

Even when the conversation turned to bridge, it continued at an elevated pitch, re-living the previous week's game when they "destroyed" the opposition.

"Remember, we got into the right contract and went for no trump?" Barbara reminisced happily.

"Oh yes," Maura said. "They thought we were going for spades." Barbara was an excellent partner and sometimes displayed an instinct that defied reason. She taught maths at the local secondary school, and this clearly stood to her. But it was some deep intuition that made her a special player. A few hundred years ago, Maura reflected, she might have been burned as a witch.

They parted shortly afterwards. Maura finished her shopping and went through the checkout towards the carpark.

After dinner, when Harold had finished with the Financial Times, and the TV news was over, Maura decided to broach the subject, trying as best she could to make light of it. When she'd finished speaking she quickly showed him the tickets and the invitations, as if these would mollify him. She felt as if she were laying tribute at the feet of a king.

"I don't believe it," he said.

"I can hardly believe it myself," she said, hoping against hope. "We deserve a break. You've been working so hard...and so have I." In the previous week she had to fight the clock to complete the annual accounts of the practice.

"That's not what I mean, Maura," he retorted angrily, standing with his back to the fireplace. "You knew my views about it." A flush appeared in his normally sallow face.

"I ... just had to do it." She raised her arms and let them fall to her sides.

"Had to? Had to? You actually appeared on that silly, demeaning quiz show." He passed a hand across his brow then straightened his spectacles which had been dislodged slightly.

"We've never been to the States," she replied. "And this ... trip..." She faltered, unable to put into words what it meant to her.

"That's not the point. You knew how I felt about it and you went behind my back. My god almighty..." He trailed off as if unable to grasp the enormity of it all.

"It's not that bad, Harold," she began in a cajoling tone. He was so easily offended. What if she'd had an affair? "Christmas in New York and New Year's Eve in Washington ... can't be bad ... all expenses paid..." She felt like a sales rep trying to talk up the merits of shoddy merchandise.

"This is cultural imperialism of the worst sort. Are we supposed to thank America for these ... these crumbs...? Besides, I was looking forward to Christmas here," he added woodenly. "You'd think I didn't provide ..."

"I work in the practice too..." She tailed off because he wasn't listening. An unsettling thought occurred to him.

"Has the programme already been shown?"

"Yes," she answered timidly.

"When?"

"Wednesday evening."

"So everyone knows. Everyone except me. Christ." Ignoring his own professional counsel, he ground his teeth. "And that of course was the evening you said you were going to bridge. I see it all now. I didn't realise you were quite so devious, Maura. I'm disappointed in you. Very disappointed." He replaced his reading glasses with the horn-rimmed ones which made him look even more stern.

She felt miserable. "I should … have been more … up front, Harold. I didn't mean…"

"You shouldn't have gone on that damn programme. You know how important credibility is in the caring professions. You work in the surgery."

She visualised the terror in children's faces as Harold bore down on them, drill in hand. He lacked a light touch and it always fell to her to try to put the kids at their ease. He was unbending, trapped in some formal image of himself.

"But think of the fun we'll have, Harold … tripping the light fantastic…" She continued for a while in that vein, trying to jolly him along.

"You, maybe," he said.

"What do you mean?"

"You surely don't think I'm going to tag along on that … that skite, in view of what you've done. Besides, there are my patients to consider."

She hadn't expected him to congratulate her

on her victory but this reaction seemed excessive. Was he about to ruin everything?

"You can get a locum. It's a holiday period," she pointed out.

"That's irrelevant. Needless to say, I don't want you to go but," he shrugged and with a pained expression continued, "I suppose in this age of liberation I can't stop you. But please don't expect me to go, or be party to this in any way." A sudden image of tabloid photographers besetting them at the airport made him shudder. The Crowther prize-winners. God in heaven.

"But Harold … the second ticket…" She was close to tears. It wasn't as if he'd been cuckolded.

"Sell the damn thing. Give it to charity. This was all your doing. I have no hand, act or part in it whatever." He made a slashing movement with his hand, closing the discussion. That was his last word on the subject.

He headed for the stairs, already loosening his tie. He had to be up at seven-thirty the next morning for his usual Sunday four-ball.

"Oh Christ." Maura sat down weakly, her carefully laid plans unravelling in front of her face. She went to the cabinet where he kept the whiskey and poured herself a large one. She drained it quickly, refilled the glass, and brought it into the kitchen where she felt more comfortable and sat at the pine table. Her flustered thoughts gradually settled into a more even flow of memory that started with her visit to Dr Chalmers about two years previously.

He had smiled kindly at her, guessing accurately the purpose of her visit.

"Is that husband of yours coming for his test?" he asked. There was an air of complicity between them which she appreciated. Even though he often played golf with Harold and was a kindred medical man, she felt that he was on her side. She shook her head sadly.

"Bloody male pride," Chalmers said in a rich Scottish accent. I come across it so many times. Unbelievable."

"Could you talk to him about it?" Maura asked. If it was a male thing, she reasoned, it would take another man to act as honest broker.

"I have done, Maura. No good. He won't face facts. Or he literally doesn't want to know." He looked closely at her. "You really want a child, don't you?"

"Yes." She might have said more but her lower lip began to tremble.

"Have you considered adoption?"

"We talked about it once but Harold isn't interested. And to be honest, I'd like to … conceive if it were possible…" She felt like a stereotype of a biological clock watcher.

"And you're both trying?" Chalmers inquired. "I mean is the old boudoir a hub of activity?"

Maura smiled despite herself. "Oh, about once a week. Saturday night…" She tailed off.

Dr. Chalmers drummed his fingers on the

desktop. Since it was doubtful if he had much to reflect on, the break in conversation was more probably due to embarrassment. He knew she trusted him to maintain professional confidentiality, and he appreciated it.

Maura came straight to the point. "What about in vitro fertilisation?"

"Well, that's a possibility," Chalmers said. "But what about Harold? Will he agree?"

"It would be his sperm … Why should be object?" She genuinely didn't know on what grounds he could object but then she didn't live inside his head.

"Maybe…" Chalmers said judiciously.

"I mean, it's not as if … you know, a sperm bank … or some anonymous donor…"

"No … no. I agree. But it is a bit more complicated than that. And I take it, you haven't discussed this with him?"

"No … I was hoping … you would."

He laughed outright. "Maura, you're a terrible woman. You're going to break up a good golf partnership before you're finished."

"But you will speak to him?"

"Yes, damn it."

And he was as good as his word. Whether he could have handled it more diplomatically she would never know. All she did know was that it back-fired badly and left her in despair. Harold had come home from his Sunday golf game and sat silent and tight-lipped all through dinner. Maura couldn't stand it, though she sensed what the issue was.

"I can't believe it," he said eventually through clenched teeth.

"What?"

"You know very well. Imagine going behind my back and telling Chalmers about … personal matters…" He let his cutlery fall with a clatter.

"He is our GP," she pointed out.

"I don't care what he is," Harold grated. "I have to meet him at the club. He button-holed me in the bloody car-park, with some daft proposition about in vitro fertilisation. I'm surprised he didn't hold out a test tube and ask for a sample right there and then…"

"But, Harold, they can do wonderful things nowadays…"

"It's a wanker's charter," he exploded. "I'm having none of it." He stormed out of the house. She had never seen such a display of melodrama on Harold's part before. What had made him such a stuffed shirt? She hadn't a clue.

That was where the matter rested for the next two years.

After her couple of whiskies Maura went into the lounge, resisted the temptation to have another drink, and lay down on the sofa where she eventually fell asleep.

Harold left the house the next morning without saying a word. His clubs, caddy car and raingear were in the boot of the Audi. He wore two Pringle sweaters against the cold and remembered to bring his golf umbrella and all-weather shoes. As he turned out of the driveway on to the main road a car fell in behind and followed him through the light suburban traffic at a discreet distance. Harold listened to the news on the car radio and when it was over he listened to some remixed big-band music. He noted that the sky did not look very encouraging but, he thought, with any luck the rain would hold off until they finished their round. He turned into the golf club, rattling across the cattle grid, and parked as close as he could to the locker rooms. He got out of the car and started to get his gear from the boot.

The Toyota parked about fifty yards away and the occupants observed him closely.

"We could do it now," the driver said.

"No," Paul said. "Later."

Patrick was silent. He studied Harold carefully. There was, he had to admit, a reasonable likeness at the level of structure – size, shape of head and features, jawline, etc. The differences were mainly cosmetic – hair colouring, complexion and skin tone. Paul was too tall and willowy. Patrick felt sure he would pick the short straw. Besides he spoke the best English, with little accent.

Emerging from the locker room, Harold went to the practice green swinging his putter. He liked to get in some practice before his friends arrived. Having got the feel of the rather damp grass and put his slightly modified grip to the test, he went to the nets to practice his long irons. His swing was too fast and abrupt, no doubt reflecting the aggravation Maura had caused him.

When Donald Chalmers arrived his worst fears were confirmed.

"You canny devil," Chalmers ribbed him. "That's some prize Maura won. Wish my wife could get me a trip like that."

Harold made no answer. He had no intention of telling Chalmers what he really felt about it. They walked to the first tee box where the other two were waiting. They of course had also heard the news and one of them had seen the show, and they were fulsome in their congratulations. The upshot was that Harold mistimed his drive and shanked the ball into a spinney to the left of the ladies' tee. He had to drop out; then he forced his next short which resulted in a vicious duck hook. The commiserating silence of his partners got under his skin. A triple bogey on the first hole was almost unheard of, especially for a twelve handicapper.

"Yes, it's a fantastic opportunity," one of the other men said as if he was trying to settle Harold down. "You could even take a side trip to Augusta."

"Great idea," Chalmers concurred. This was the Mecca. Amen corner, manicured fairways, golden-sanded bunkers, island greens with subtle contours. The images conjured up made them play better, except for Harold who continued hacking like a novice.

"Easy for them," Harold thought. "They don't know the full story." He had had to put his foot down; Maura had given him no option. He wondered if she would really go without him. If she did he would have to book into some hotel for Christmas. Since a boiled egg was beyond his culinary abilities, a turkey was completely out of the question. He thought of himself sitting forlornly at a table for one in a festive dining room, surrounded by happy couples and families, and felt a surge of anger mixed with self-pity. But he couldn't relent, not after the way she'd ignored his advice and gone behind his back.

Perversely, the feeling of self-pity served to slow down his swing and he began to make better contact with the ball, but there was no way he could make up the accumulated deficit of the first six holes. And although his long game improved, his putting let him down. On the tenth he funked a tiddler of a putt and left the ball on the lip of the hole. He stared at it for a long time, hoping for an earthquake, while Chalmers tried to console him by saying, "I saw Tiger do that on the Fourth in St. Andrews."

No one, of course, asked Harold what was wrong with him. These golfers preferred to talk about safely objective things like the British Open, the Masters, the imminent turkey competitions during which each golfer hoped to bag a bird for the table and bring it home with all the pride of an ancestral hunter. A light sleety drizzle began to fall; the players opened their umbrellas and put on their raingear. They played on grimly, trying to prevent the rain-soaked clubs from swivelling in their hands. The balls began to plug in the fairways, and lifting was not allowed. Harold wanted to go in but it just wasn't done, unless there was a consensus.

He was glad when they finally reached the eighteenth. His drive was a daisy-cutter that never properly got airborne and only went about a hundred yards. It didn't matter anymore; it was too late for honour to be saved. What had gotten into her, he wondered. She wasn't even a good traveller. That holiday to the Canaries had given her a sick tummy that lasted a whole week. Early menopause perhaps? He doubted it, though couldn't rule out something of a hormonal nature.

The game had been a wash-out in more ways than one. After a shower in the locker room and a quick drink in the bar, he bade farewell to his friends and went out to his car. As he drove out through the gate, he surfed the radio for a news bulletin but only came up with a studio discussion, the theme of which appeared to be the tendency for all politicians to flock to the centre of the spectrum. Can't be bad for the middle classes, Harold thought, as he listened vaguely to the heated exchanges. Suddenly, a strange voice intruded; it didn't come from the radio and seemed to be directed at him. He felt something cold against the back of his neck. Half-turning, he glimpsed a balaclava and a gun.

"Don't turn around again," the voice said. Harold lost control of the car for an instant and fought to regain it. His hands were so numb he could hardly feel the steering wheel.

"Turn left at the next intersection."

"I've … no money…" He couldn't catch his breath. This couldn't be happening. It was a normal golf day.

"…the Labour Party has lost its identity completely…" the radio continued. "The rot began all those years ago with so-called New Labour…"

"Switch that off. Turn left … left. Here!"

Harold obeyed both commands as best he could. He cornered widely then overcorrected.

"Straight on for about three kilometres." The voice was slightly accented. But he couldn't place it.

"I think … you've made…" Harold began.

"Don't talk."

He felt the pressure of the gun against the base of his skull. It was cold and brutal. His vision was blurred, forcing him to drive slowly. A few minutes later he was told to stop and was transferred to the waiting Toyota by two other men. He was blindfolded and his hands were tied behind his back. He heard another car being driven away, probably his own.

He summoned up enough courage to say, "You must … a mistake … I'm … just a dentist…"

"No mistake. Keep quiet."

The effect of the blindfold compounded his fear and he gagged several times. It was impossible to relate time and distance. He had the impression they were travelling fast but the sound of the revs seemed to belie that. There was a smell of garlic in the car which confirmed his suspicion that his abductors were foreign. They didn't talk among themselves which suggested that things were going according to some plan. After some indeterminate period of time he lurched to the right as the car turned abruptly. Then the going got rougher as if they were travelling along a rutted dirt road.

When the car eventually came to a stop he was bundled out and led into some kind of derelict building. He could smell damp and rotting timbers and something like old manure or silage. At one point a floor board splintered under his foot. A hand on his shoulder forced him down a flight of stone steps. He was pushed through a doorway, the lintel grazing his head. After a few more steps he was lowered into a sitting position on some kind of bench. His hands were untied and the blindfold removed. Just as his eyes became accustomed to the dark he saw two figures leave the cellar. Then he heard the door being bolted on the outside.

"I've been kidnapped," he thought. The realisation overwhelmed him. "Jesus … I've been kidnapped," he said aloud. He started to shake.

CHAPTER 5

THOUGH NOT PARTICULARLY given to flights of fancy, Lawrence did at least let his mind wander as they circled Reagan Airport waiting for landing permission. Every time the pilot crossed the Potomac and veered towards the Mall there was a split-second view of the Capitol Building. He wondered if Evelyn enjoyed the trappings of power and all of the deference and envy that went with it. Not having a ready answer to that question was strange in a way since they had once been very close, and could almost finish each other's sentences. One thing he was fairly sure of, however, was that she was not in love with Stanley Ralston, even if his Congressional and Committee plumes lent him some glamour.

When he thought of Evelyn the years dissolved. They were back in the school yard again, he in one corner, she in another, too young and gauche to meet, yet acutely conscious of each other's presence. One glance of her brown eyes expressed an intimacy that seemed to be directed solely at him. "We both know, don't we?" was what those eyes used to say to him. It was inconceivable that any other boy would be allowed to read that message.

They grew up in a suburb of San Francisco. Although he was one grade ahead she was more mature, and when they hit the white water of puberty it was she who gave direction to the next phase of their relationship. They went for long intense walks, hardly talking, barely touching for fear of altering, or jeopardising in some way, their former innocent friendship. When, finally, sex entered the picture, as it was fated to do, infatuation quickly followed. They discovered, no, created, something special. The constellation of circumstances that ultimately drove her away from him was still a mystery. Of course he had been aware, acutely aware, of the facts but not what they had meant to her. Partly because of that he had never really blamed her for marrying Stanley Ralston who was then the class nerd and now the bought-and-paid-for congressman and CASA Chairman. Over the years Lawrence had financed Stanley's political campaigns. Only the cognoscenti knew where the real power lay and Lawrence preferred it that way. America was run by its giant corporations whose executives used politicians as front men and flak-catchers.

Maybe it was partly Evelyn's rejection of him that spurred Lawrence on to succeed in business. Of course he had been lucky too. Shortly after he'd taken over his father's business, the Vietnam War increased the demand for conventional armaments by a factor of ten at least. He was not asleep at the switch when that happened; far from it. He borrowed up to the hilt to gear up the plant. He forged important contacts in the Pentagon. Some years later he played the financial markets and quadrupled his own net worth in as many years. Then his marriage of convenience to Amanda, whose father owned a chain of drug stores up and down the West coast, put the capstone on his corporate existence. She also had very useful contacts in the business world, including Wall Street.

From the very beginning he made it a priority to glad-hand the politicians. His father – and grandfather – had always told him that was how the system worked, and the strategy had certainly paid off. Deep down, of course, he disliked politicians because of their hypocrisy, but he liked the role of puppet-master which gradually grew into one of king-maker. He had been indispensable to Stanley during the latter's gubernatorial campaign in California in the 'nineties and had pulled out all the stops for him a decade later during his campaign for the Congress. Stanley owed him a lot of favours even though he had already put many Federal contracts his way.

It was the Iraq War that put Kaltronics on the map. Every TV programme that showed a direct hit by a smart missile on an Iraqi target was an advertisement of inestimable value for Kaltronics. Those missiles that didn't perform so well, the ones that caused major collateral change, never featured in the broadcasts because of selective, Pentagon-directed editing. The wars in Afghanistan and Syria had also been extremely profitable and had burned off most of the unwanted inventory. Kaltronics was now among the top ten companies in the States and was quoted on all the exchanges and bourses in the world, though Lawrence, of course, retained control – and wouldn't have it any other way.

The jet passed the Mall one more time on a lower trajectory. The Vietnam Memorial was barely visible, reflecting the ambivalence of how to celebrate a defeat, or at least a non-victory. Because of his age Lawrence had no recollection of that war but, having read about it, often wished that precision weaponry had been available to the US back then.

"Starting to make our approach now, sir," the pilot announced over the intercom. Lawrence tidied up his papers and fastened the seat belt.

It was Lawrence who suggested a stroll around the grounds of Stanley's well-appointed home in Bethesda; he needed to stretch his legs after the flight. Both men wore overcoats. Some years earlier a deranged derelict had fired shots through the railings and ever since then security had been tightened. Heavy-set men now patrolled the perimeter, trying to be as unobtrusive as possible. It seemed appropriate somehow; Stanley had always been cosseted even as a kid.

"Anything on your mind, Lawrence?" Stanley asked, pulling up his coat collar. He was not an outdoor man. Nor did he feel altogether comfortable with Lawrence. They had a lot of history together in which Evelyn had featured significantly, though there were other things besides.

Lawrence told him that the 'big project' was going more or less to plan though not all of the financing was yet in place. Stanley seemed content and asked if there was anything else to be discussed.

"Well, a couple of items," Lawrence answered. "The Pentagon hasn't come back to me on the tender for the new Patriot missiles."

"It's such a bureaucracy," Stanley replied with an affected groan. "Still, I might be able to make some inquiries."

Lawrence gave him a sideways glance; he was unimpressed and a little surprised by the word, 'might'. Was it possible that Stanley was trying to strike out on his own, become his own man, albeit rather late in the day? He let it pass for the moment. "Then there's the whole geo-political scene." He simply flagged the subject, leaving it to Stanley to develop the theme as he wished. It was important for Lawrence to have the Administration's thinking on broad strategic issues; otherwise Kaltronics would have to do its long-range planning in a vacuum. His father had, for example, missed the Glasnost turning point all those years ago, and that could have been disastrous since it changed the basic parameters of the arms race. Fortunately, Kaltronics had not invested too heavily in nuclear armaments, and were able to re-orient towards high-tech conventional weaponry. In fact, they had been able to steal a march on those companies which had bought into Reagan's mind-blowing vision of Star Wars. In the immediate aftermath of Glasnost, however, there was a real danger that defence expenditure would be slashed. It took all the clout of Stanley's Congressional Committee (CASA), the military and the arms industry, to make sure that that didn't happen. Stanley had dithered for a while until he realised where his best interests lay. The so-called end of history was scuppered when the twin towers were attacked. Pre-emptive defence was music to the ears of the arms industries.

"Some of the Agencies want to cosy up with Russia," Stanley remarked. "On the grounds that there's no point in twisting the knife. Others aren't so sure. I guess there's not much real analysis being done – CASA is taking a breather at the moment."

The 'castor man', Lawrence thought; he could be pushed in any direction. Politicians were all alike, leading from behind. When they said 'analysis', they really meant 'polls'. Public opinion was their only reality. Moulding it was beyond them, certainly beyond Stanley. And yet, truth be told, wasn't it his very malleability that made him so useful? Adaptive plasticity was what the shrinks called it, and Stanley was full of it.

Lawrence wanted to get to more topical and immediate issues. "Can you count on continued borrowing from China?" he inquired.

"I think so. The alternative would be to cut the arms budget. And I can't see the President going for that." Stanley hesitated for a while, hands sunk deep in the pockets of his coat.

"Or your fellow Republicans," Lawrence offered.

"No, I guess not. We've already diverted aid funds into the arms budget. So that's a straw in the wind."

"Too bad about Africa," Lawrence said.

"Well, the dark continent has no political clout any more. They never used the aid properly, anyway. A lot of it ended up in the Swiss bank accounts of dictators."

Lawrence was aware of the switch from aid to arms; some months ago he'd discussed it with the Secretary of State. When dealing with Stanley it was always desirable to get a second opinion.

"Look, you have to improve competitiveness with China and reduce the Budget deficit. The best way of achieving both objectives without cutting back on armaments is to devalue the dollar by ten or fifteen percent. Take my advice. The Treasury is likely to go for it. And with the present configuration on the Hill it wouldn't take much to get a majority in both Houses."

"You make a good pitch, I grant you that. We'll take it under advisement."

This academic, laid-back response got under Lawrence's skin. He would have to set other wheels in motion to get Stanley to take a stand. He also needed to remind him of the facts of life.

"I take it you're considering running again?"

"Absolutely, I have to complete my programme."

"You can count on our support," Lawrence said, "You'll need a full war chest."

"We're very grateful, Lawrence. And we don't forget our friends."

The plurals grated on Lawrence's nerves. Was this vain, ineffectual man, who relied on spin doctors to give him a persona, getting ahead of himself? That was the question Lawrence brought with him as they went indoors to discuss some other matters over a drink.

From an upstairs window Evelyn had seen him walking in the grounds with Stanley. When they went indoors she decided to give them some time to discuss whatever business they had on their agenda. While she waited she changed her clothes and re-applied her make-up. Then she went downstairs and made an entrance, disregarding her husband's sensitivities.

Lawrence rose to greet her and resumed his seat only when she sat.

"Being the wife of the nation's most influential congressman has been good to you, Evelyn," Lawrence said as if they hadn't met in years.

"Because or in spite of?" She looked banteringly from one man to the other but it wasn't entirely clear just how light-hearted her comment was meant to be. "First Lady would, of course be better," she added.

"Oh, I don't know," Lawrence said. "From my reading of the media you upstage her in many ways."

She laughed pleasantly. "I hope I'm not interrupting any great affairs of state."

"We've had our chat," Stanley said with little grace.

"And has it been of benefit to the nation or to you?" she inquired.

"Both." Lawrence grinned. "There's often a mutuality of interests."

"Indeed." She accepted her usual dry martini from the butler. From the French doors of the conservatory she could see a groom walking the horses, including her own chestnut mare. It would be wonderful to go riding with

Lawrence but she doubted if he would have time for that.

"We don't see enough of you," she said to Lawrence. "Remember, *mi casa es su casa*." This was a variant of the well-used pun on the acronym of Stanley's committee.

"Thank you kindly. But, you know, the demands of business…"

"Don't you ever relax?" She asked, knowing that he never did and probably never could.

"I think I've forgotten how. Sad but true." Lawrence spread his large hands in a gesture of surrender.

"And how is your wife … Amanda isn't it?"

"Oh, away as usual. The Caribbean I think."

Stanley watched them both, not seeming to notice how often Evelyn touched Lawrence's arm as she spoke.

She hoped that her husband would be called away to one of his many duties but it wasn't to be. In fact it was Lawrence who had to leave first.

"Foiled again," she thought as he made his departure with the usual ritual of promises to keep in touch and not be a stranger. Maybe she had screwed up her life to date. But it wasn't over yet.

She consoled herself with the thought that he was bound to be at the New Year's Ball which was only a matter of weeks away. She could surely escape her official duties for a while and put in an appearance. Yes, it would be a golden opportunity, risky but golden. And there would have to be a resolution. She could not allow more unproductive time to slide by without resolving this ever-present affair of the heart.

She knew that Lawrence was not perfect; in fact, he was almost a caricature of that entrepreneurial type driven by, and fixated on, the bottom line. But that made him purposeful, a force of nature. Even at high school when the diffidence of the early teens had worn off, he had pursued her in a forthright, manly way without fear of rebuff. She knew that she had been standoffish and that made other boys keep their distance. But not Lawrence. He took the plunge – admittedly after she had given a subtle signal – and they dated regularly, became an item. He pressed her for sex but not unduly and it wasn't until Prom night that she consented. He was considerate; she doubted if it was his first time and had reason to believe he'd had something going with an older woman. It was an exhilarating experience and, despite the passage of time, she could vividly recall the events and feelings of the encounter. Although sex got better and better after that, her clearest recollection was of the first time – cramped in the back of a Ford Mustang, some fishing gear of his father's sticking into her back.

Later on she went to Bryn Mawr and he to Harvard, to study languages and engineering, respectively. They met regularly, especially during the vacations. It was tacitly assumed that they would marry and when he proposed – on her twenty-second birthday – she was ecstatic though not all that surprised.

The surprise was to come later when her parents, especially her father, took a very poor view of the match. Her father, a third generation Anglo-American, as near to the archetypal Wasp as made no difference, had always been civil to Lawrence when he called for her. Perhaps he believed in reverse psychology. But when marriage was mooted, objections were lodged in no uncertain terms. Since class was hardly the issue, Evelyn could only conclude that some latent ethnic prejudice had come to the surface. She was shaken to the core and staggered by her parent's preference – revealed later – for Stanley Ralston, whose father was a key figure in the Masonic Lodge. Evelyn knew Stanley at school and she had met him intermittently when she visited Lawrence at Harvard. She had even gone out with him a couple of times to help him out when he had been stood up by some other girl. But there was no more to it than that. She certainly hadn't encouraged him in any way. So when she was confronted by the dreadful old-fashioned mandarin proposition by her father she reacted badly.

"What have you got against Lawrence?" she had demanded. "He's an American. Just like you are."

"You don't understand these things," her father said infuriatingly. "You're too young."

"I'm old enough to be screwing him," she countered furiously.

"Evelyn!" her mother cried. "How dare you…"

Her father stormed out, ashen-faced. Later he called Lawrence and told him that under no circumstances could he give his approval to the marriage. He told him that Evelyn was going to marry Stanley Ralston.

Predictably, though unwisely, Lawrence bearded him in his den and a tense scene ensued. Her father tried to calm him down by saying it was nothing personal but this had the opposite effect on Lawrence who called him a bigoted old fart who lived in the past. Evelyn trembled. She'd never seen Lawrence lose his temper before. In a way she admired him for taking on her father but the lack of subtlety was all too apparent.

"Get out of this house immediately," her father shouted, having completely lost his composure for possibly the first time in his life.

"Come with me now!" Lawrence said to Evelyn. "We'll never set foot in this house again."

Evelyn looked at her mother weeping silently and she hesitated. She would have had little compunction about walking out on her father, who was a strict disciplinarian, and opinionated to an unreasonable degree. But her mother was different and she had suffered enough during her married life. It was all too sudden, too abrupt. She needed time to think. So she hesitated, and collapsed into tears. Lawrence asked her once more to leave with him and when he got no answer he stormed out of the house.

Evelyn thought that in time she might be able to mend fences but Lawrence was more pig-headed than she realised. He insisted on eloping immediately, whereas she pleaded for more time. A few weeks later he took up with another girl and paraded her around. Even though Evelyn saw through the ploy she did feel jealous. But she also began to wonder about Lawrence's impetuosity; it wasn't quite such an admirable quality when it was directed against her.

Her father rubbed it in. "You see now, Evelyn, what a bully he is. Be grateful that you had the opportunity to see him in his true colours. You could have made a dreadful mistake."

Evelyn held her peace; she didn't see Lawrence as a bully but more like a bull in a china shop. He couldn't compromise; it just wasn't in him. Out of an equal measure of spite she took up with Stanley, though in a casual way. Lawrence was scathing about this.

"How could you go out with that creep?" he demanded. "I thought you had some standards."

"What about your Swedish meatball?" she retorted, flushed and angry.

"She knows what she wants," Lawrence said. "And she goes for it."

"Just like you."

"You get one chance in life," he said with unexpected gravity. "If you hesitate you lose. One chance, that's all there is."

She had the sensation of a door closing, the bolt being driven home. It was over. Her father had fired the shot but Lawrence had turned it into a fatal wound.

Now with the benefit of hindsight and whatever wisdom she might have acquired over the years, she knew that she'd never really gotten Lawrence out of her system. He had been too strong-willed and impulsive for her at the wrong time. He took no prisoners. Life with him would have had the force of a hurricane, unless of course he'd mellowed over the years. But she doubted if he had.

He hadn't married the Swedish girl, but a sophisticated debutante, Amanda Brent, who was wealthy in her own right. From the odd media piece she inferred that it was basically a marriage of convenience, not unlike her own. There was some strange and compelling symmetry about that which intrigued her. It was as if both of the principals were marking time, waiting for a final resolution, that second chance that he had ruled out. Maybe it was up to her to make it happen.

They had met a number of times over the years and managed to hit the sheets on three occasions. These fleeting encounters served only to strengthen her desire for a more permanent arrangement.

She often wondered if Lawrence's manipulation of Stanley was in part motivated by a desire to show him up as a weakling. Of course the overt reason was a business one: Government contracts and a say in policy. But still … two birds with one stone. That would be perfectly consistent with Lawrence's efficiency drive. A hundred birds if he could manage it, with half a pebble.

Lawrence remained in her thoughts as she went over the seating arrangement for a formal dinner that night. She suggested some changes but, as usual, the Chief of Protocol had various abstruse reasons why these would not be appropriate. She wondered why the hell he had sought her advice in the first place.

———

At eight o'clock that evening Maura began to worry. It wasn't like Harold to miss his evening meal even if he was in a sulk. And he didn't spend too long on the 19th hole when he had the car with him; he was cautious about most things but especially about the humiliation of being caught for drunk-driving. Maybe he was punishing her but had he not done enough of that by refusing to travel with her to the States? She had put his dinner near the microwave where she could quickly re-heat it when he showed up. It was strange that he hadn't called to say he'd be late; he was normally considerate about things like that.

Just before ten the landline rang. She put the receiver to her ear and heard an accented, low-pitched voice, stating what could have been the most normal and bland fact in the world.

"We have your husband."

"What…?

"Your husband has been taken hostage."

Maura's immediate reaction was to laugh. This was Hertfordshire and Harold was … well, Harold. But this reaction was quickly replaced by its opposite.

"Who is this …?" Her hands flew to her throat. A sick prank? No, her instinct told her.

"Just listen. He's safe for the moment."

"How do I know …?"

Then she heard Harold's strangled voice which seemed to come from far away, "Do what they ask, Maura … Whatever … Do it…"

"Harold…" It was no use; he'd gone. The other voice came on the line.

"If you need further proof you'll find his car outside the station nearest to Hertingfordbury. Do not mention this to anybody, especially the police, if you want to see him alive again."

"What … do you want?" Her panic grew. She didn't have access to funds – apart from the few thousand in prize money which was of no consequence.

"I will meet you at noon tomorrow. King's Cross station. Come on your own. If you fail to show you will seal your husband's death warrant." The line went dead.

She was trembling, trying to absorb the sudden onslaught. She still held the receiver in her hand.

This was no hallucination. But what in god's name did it all mean? Who would want to kidnap Harold … unless he had a fortune stashed away. That would mean he had been leading a double life. She was almost prepared to believe anything. But if there was money stashed away, it was obviously well hidden, so how was she supposed to locate it to pay a ransom? Confused and shocked, she didn't know how frightened she ought to be. Yet he was in mortal danger. That much seemed certain. What had he gotten himself into? Were they Arab terrorists? She didn't know. Nothing was clear. Strange that they hadn't demanded money. Not yet at any rate. What then was the ransom?

She looked at the wallpaper opposite the telephone table in the hall. Harold had never liked the pattern, those little red buds, but she hadn't had much choice, being on a strict budget. The headlights of a neighbour's car moving slowly outside shone through the fanlight, played across the ceiling and through the banisters. Harold kidnapped … what in god's name were they talking about?

CHAPTER 6

AT TIMES EVELYN had to pinch herself to realise that she was a celebrity, virtually a role model for women across the States. At other times she felt as if the whole deal was some sort of cosmetic scam which required her merely to wear nice clothes and behave in a ladylike manner. She frequently oscillated between those magnetic poles. On this particular day she was, comfortably, somewhere in the middle, just going about her business which happened to involve talking to the students of a public school in Virginia about the evils of drug-taking, especially opioids. She had taught for a large part of her life, albeit in a parochial school, and was fairly relaxed standing in front of these freshly scrubbed students. The teachers sat in a semi-circle behind her, smiling and applauding frequently. They were the *claquers* who initiated each and every ovation.

So warm was the reception that she almost believed she was delivering a magnificent and original speech. They were of course in a way applauding Stanley's office not her. She sometimes wondered, more frequently of late, whether Stanley could distinguish between his office and himself as a person. She at least tried to keep her feet on the ground but it was hard

going at times. Whenever she went out in
public people often approached her, shook her
warmly by the hand and asked for her
autograph – rather diffidently as if they didn't
really want to treat her as a movie star. She also
had to dress formally – at least as well as the
First Lady, against whom she was inclined to
benchmark herself – and while she appreciated
haute couture, she sometimes felt it to be an
encroachment on her freedom. Gone were the
days when she could schlepp around in jeans
and sweater. To date, the networks, social
media and tabloids had been reasonably kind to
her, except for one blogger – probably a
Democrat – who asserted that she had as little
substance as her husband.

As she neared the end of her talk she
wondered if her words would make any
difference to the lives of those multiracial kids.
From some of them, especially the heavies at
the back of the hall, she could almost feel the
waves of disaffection rolling towards her. To
them she was probably just a diversion at best.
She doubted if her carefully rehearsed parables
and slogans would keep any of them off drugs.
For underprivileged kids toughness was their
only claim to fame. And that could best be
achieved by taking on all-comers, parents,
teachers, authority figures and the law. By
proving themselves in this way they also,
unfortunately, began the process of damaging
themselves.

She answered the few questions that had probably been planted, and then had the mandatory cup of coffee with the teachers in the staff room. She was struck, not for the first time, by how in their polite and rather strained chit-chat, they scrupulously avoided political issues. Some years earlier she had assumed that this was because people didn't expect her to be *au fait* with the issues of the day and wanted to save her embarrassment. But now, with more experience under her belt, she felt there was a deeper reason, one which she could more easily accept, namely, that people didn't want to trouble her. It was perhaps a form of politesse. She could almost hear the head teacher's team talk before she arrived. "...and for god's sake, don't button-hole the woman about her husband's Committee or the situation in Syria. She can't be blamed for his policies."

The teachers were kind to a fault, and when, finally, she bade them farewell they thanked her effusively and accompanied her out to the waiting limousine. Maybe she'd made a few people happy for a passing moment. You couldn't say that about many jobs, not even teaching, and certainly not her internship in the Department of Commerce, where, as a middle-ranking civil servant, she was given very little responsibility for anything of substance. At least now, she could sprinkle a little fairy dust around at her discretion.

On the journey back her driver asked how it

had gone.

"Well enough, Edgar, although I'm not sure if any of those kids were really listening to me."

"Probably not," he said with a laugh. He was becoming much too familiar, she thought.

Crossing Key Bridge she noticed how fast-flowing the river was and how it broiled around the many dangerously protruding rocks. It was a wild, almost savage river, not the kind you would expect to find flowing through a modern cosmopolitan city. The Indian name, Potomac, seemed appropriate. She could see Georgetown students jogging along the canal path. Though not disenchanted with her time of life, she did envy the youthful freedom of those students.

It was one of those rare, reception-free evenings when she and Stanley could have had a nice dinner together. It didn't work out like that, however. He had sandwiches and coffee brought to him in his office while she picked at a salad in the kitchen, the chef having tried his best to tempt her to something more substantial.

They did meet briefly later on in the drawing room and she asked him about his day.

"I didn't have a lot on today," he said. "Well, apart from Lawrence's visit. Things are beginning to wind down for Thanksgiving and Christmas, I guess."

She fetched a lighter from the mantelpiece of the Adam's fireplace and lit one of the three cigarettes she allowed herself in the evenings.

Reflexively, he waved the smoke away.

"We have to start gearing up for the next election." He sighed as if it were a matter of duty rather than of volition.

"So you've decided?" She knew he had been thinking about it.

"I think so, I'm under a lot of pressure … moral pressure … from the Party."

"I can imagine." She had an inkling that he would become an empty shell out of office. And it was doubtful if the extra time they would have together would do much to strengthen their marriage which, though never exactly robust, had in recent years become little more than a charade. She sometimes thought of a quip directed against a corrupt Senator: He does to the country what he should be doing to his wife. For Stanley the only reality was politics; it absorbed all of his time and energy. Maybe it was just as well they never had children. She had seen too many kids of other political families go off the rails.

"You might," she said at length, "ask me where I stand on this."

"Well," he turned to face her. "How do you feel about it?"

She thought for a while though she didn't really have to. For all her ambivalence about the nature of her duties, she was hooked on the job, almost as much as he was.

"OK," she said. "I'm OK with it."

"Fine," he replied as if that put even more

pressure on him to stand again. He went out to meet William, the deputy chairman of his Committee. Evelyn watched TV for a while.

A little later on she got a call on her phone from a close friend and journalist, Lillian Bartok.

"Hello Lil."

"Can you do me the honour …?"

"Cut it out."

"Can we meet?" Lillian asked. "I know it's a bit late but…"

"Well, an hour won't kill me." Evelyn knew she'd have to be careful with Lillian, who took her journalistic duties seriously. "Neutral ground. Your place?" She didn't want to invite Lillian too often to the house. The other hacks would suspect preferential treatment. Also, William was paranoid about press leaks and he didn't like anyone upstaging Stanley.

They met in Lillian's apartment in Georgetown, which occupied the top floor of a brownstone house.

"I've been letting this breathe." Lillian poured two large measures of bourbon. Her red Medusa-like hair fell about her face, which still carried a freckle or two.

Evelyn looked around the apartment. "Where's that toy boy of yours? Boyd isn't it?" Lillian had cradle-snatched a medical student from Georgetown University and given him board and lodging. She didn't like to sleep alone.

"You remembered his name. I'm impressed. I've let him off the leash for to-night," she laughed. "He's at a stag party."

"So what's up?" It was obvious that Lillian was on to a story. The colour of her cheeks almost matched that of the terracotta chimney breast.

Lillian sat opposite her on a futon. "Now you know I would never want to compromise you in any way."

"Perish the thought," Evelyn said with a withering look.

"Off the record, OK?"

"Why can't we chat just like we used to?" Evelyn sighed. Being a congressman's wife seemed to prevent normal friendships. And yet she didn't want to give up her status. Strange. It bore thinking about. Lillian was as good a friend as she ever had or was likely to have, and she resented the fact of not being able to share confidences whenever she felt the need.

"Do you want to go on the record?" Lillian grinned over her glass.

"I most certainly do not. I shouldn't even be here. Look, Lil, I don't really know all that much about what's going on. You know what Stanley is like. He choked the parrot."

"Well he does tend to use William a lot, almost as a press secretary. Horses for courses I guess. We're doled out morsels of information and it is almost impossible to put the whole story together…"

They discussed the Patriot Act for a while and the ways in which it had shredded individual freedoms, previously guaranteed by the Constitution. An American citizen could be picked up and jailed without any justification apart from a vague suspicion of treason. They returned to the question of an overall strategy.

"Maybe there isn't one," Evelyn said. "Maybe they just make it up as they go along. Ad hockery, you know."

"I thought so too, but recently I've been getting vibes which suggest that there may, just may, be something big in the works. Look, suppose I lay it all out for you then you can decide whether you want to give a reaction or not. Any kind of reaction, hunch, feeling, anything." Lillian leant forward, an earnest expression on her face. "Is that OK?"

"Shoot," Evelyn said. "But, remember, I don't know much and I'm not a quisling."

"Of course not. All right. I've got a contact in State, a bit of a bleeding-heart liberal but reliable enough." Lillian paused to light a cigarette and watch the smoke gently fade away. "It seems that US aid is being pulled out of Africa and other needy countries. And we're not sure what's behind it?" She looked keenly at Evelyn who shrugged.

"I don't know."

"And if you did?"

"I sure as hell wouldn't tell you." They both laughed. "What's your theory? You always have one."

"To start with, the deep state does exist, and it is determined to strengthen the American Empire – by force if necessary. The US now has a virtual monopoly in the manufacture of smart weapons. But there's no point in just stock-piling them. They have to be used, or sold, to keep the arms manufacturers in business…"

"I hope you're not suggesting that America wages war just to use up its weapons and create a demand for more?"

"That's not the only reason," Lillian admitted, "but it may well be an important one. Oil is another powerful motivator. The invasions of Iraq and Afghanistan were highly suspect. Protection of Israel and fear of Islamic fundamentalists are also in play."

Evelyn didn't disagree. She remembered being shocked to learn that the US had over nine hundred military bases around the world. If that did not indicate an imperial reach, nothing did. "So what's new?" she asked.

"Two things. The first is that the empire is being shaped and run to a much greater extent by big business. Second, there is a rumour that Kaltronics is researching a radically new weapons system, based on Nikola Tesla's earlier work. It would give the US military full-spectrum dominance over the rest of the world, especially if it included the weaponisation of space. Wall Street is playing its part, and is keen on using this new power against Iran."

"It's all a bit far-fetched…" Evelyn said with as much confidence as she could muster. She noticed that Lillian's face had taken on an almost feverish glow, although this was due in part to the flickering heat of the log fire. "I haven't heard President Trump indicate any of this."

"Look, Evelyn. The President is just a figurehead. It is the military and industrial complex that is driving this. Trump may go along with it. But if he doesn't, it won't make any difference. It is the deep state that calls the shots." Lillian sat back on the couch as if she needed a breather.

"This is a lot … to take in," Evelyn said. "And you have no evidence…"

"No hard evidence," Lillian corrected her. "But it's fairly well known that the Kaltronics Corporation has been borrowing hand over fist. That information has been around Wall Street for some time. We know that Kaltronics has hardly ever made a move in the past without a big pay-off being guaranteed in advance."

Evelyn went hot and cold. Were they two of the principal players she'd seen walking in the grounds of her home so recently – and on previous occasions too?

"I don't have to draw you a picture?" Lillian pressed.

"No," Evelyn conceded reluctantly, staring into the fireplace as if the dancing flames might conjure up some answers. Then she said quite bluntly, "OK, it's no secret that Lawrence Dwyer helped Stanley get elected. At least we know that, within these four walls. But don't demonise him…"

"Who?" Lillian interrupted.

"I don't follow…"

"Which of the two should we not demonise?"

"Both … either." Evelyn realised with a start that she'd meant Lawrence. But she had a sudden spurt of anxiety. His single-mindedness could be alarming even if well-intentioned. She knew only too well how he rushed his fences oblivious of consequences. At high school she remembered the football coach taking him out of an important game because he was a danger to himself as well as the other players. It was doubtful if he had changed.

Lillian's face had lost something of its bloom; she suddenly seemed tired. "If only part of this scenario is true, think of the suffering that's going to be inflicted on the world and on our own ninety-nine percenters. Think about it."

By now Evelyn sensed that there was more to this discussion than met the eye. Her friend could be devious at times. "You knew all along that I couldn't answer your questions. You're not really looking for information or hunches are you?"

"We-e-ell." Lillian made a see-sawing

motion with her hand.

"Then what?" Evelyn had guessed but she wanted confirmation.

"There's only one person who is close to both of the major actors."

"Christ Almighty … cut it out."

"You know I'm right." Lillian was imperturbable.

"What influence could I possibly have? I talk to students, swan about at receptions and wear the right clothes."

"You're in the right place at the right time. You don't have to ride on anyone's coat tails. Empower yourself."

"Ah, empowerment," Evelyn said with a short hollow laugh. "You're going to say something about 'nurturing' next."

"Yes. And why not?" Lillian got up and paced. "Men are incomplete. I know it sounds twee, but the feminine principle is needed to balance the goddamn species."

"Don't lay this on me," Evelyn said.

"Think about it. *Noblesse oblige.* There's no one else. Promise me you'll at least think about it."

"All right." She held up her hands, palms to the fore, indicating that Lillian should not pressure her further.

When Evelyn got into bed that night with her cold cream on and her consciousness raised, she didn't feel exactly like an Earth mother. In fact she felt annoyed that Lillian had tried to pass the chalice to her. No doubt Lillian was now sleeping peacefully in her bed or coupling with her toy boy, while Evelyn would have to contemplate that damn silly chandelier for the next several hours as she wrestled with her thoughts.

Stanley was probably already asleep in his own room. He had lost interest in her shortly after he took over the chairmanship of CASA and she had moved out of the master bedroom a little while after that. It was the night when, in what was obviously a sex dream, he had called out a man's name, 'Bill'. She was irritated by the incident even though it was probably just a subconscious reference to some teen-age experiment carried out when the world was young.

Evelyn lay on her back for a while thinking about what Lillian had said. Where was democracy in all of this? Sometimes the rhetoric from politicians amazed her. She had heard Stanley utter marvellous phrases like 'Trust the people' or 'Democracy is our only safeguard of justice and freedom'. But what was the reality? The gap between words and deeds was widening daily. She knew enough about history to realise that empires run by the rich and powerful exploited their subject people without mercy. Damn Lillian! Did she really think the wife of a congressman and former lover of an arms manufacturer could influence anything? Dream on. She fumbled in a drawer of the bedside table for a sleeping pill.

CHAPTER 7

HAROLD WOKE STIFF with fear and cold. As he wiped his eyes, he took in his surroundings: a damp cellar like a catacomb with old timber shelves and rotten roof beams from which a few rusted tenterhooks hung. On one of the shelves there were some shrivelled apples like shrunken heads. A few discoloured flagstones covered one corner of the earthen floor; elsewhere were patches of moss and fungus.

Someone had left a glass of milk and a loaf of bread near the bench on which he lay. He couldn't face it. His bowels loosened and he used the galvanised bucket that stood on the flagstones. The stench was horrible and there was nothing he could do about it. He tried to eat some of the dry bread to bind himself up. His pulse rate was dangerously high. He lay back on the bench trying to calm himself.

Why him? Why? It made no sense. If there was a ransom demand, Maura wouldn't be able to raise it. His funds were locked up in equities, unit trusts and gilts – all in his name. This now was the price of his caution and secrecy. He would have to make them understand there were no ready funds, but what if they didn't believe him?

He noticed that the brickwork surrounding

the only window was cracked and crumbling. If he were younger he might consider ways of trying to escape but at his age it would be foolhardy in the extreme. His fear began to give way to anger. Who the hell were they? Some latter-day lunatic hippies or just plain criminals? They had no right to deprive him of his freedom, threaten his very existence. Apart from the bucket he had no toilet facilities. He could already smell his own stale sweat and feel plaque beginning to form on his teeth. Gum disease couldn't be far away. Who were they?

For one fleeting moment he heard a snatch of conversation overhead through cracks in the floorboards. But he couldn't decipher it. Trapped, deprived of any semblance of dignity, he realised how heinous a crime it was, even if they stopped short of maiming or killing him. But even that was far from certain.

He sat up abruptly as he heard a bolt being drawn back. A figure in a balaclava stood hunched in the doorway.

"Why…?" Harold blurted out.

"You'll be told in time," the man said in a foreign accent, "if you co-operate."

"There's … no money. You've made … a mistake."

"No mistake." The man produced an iPhone and took a photograph of Harold. Then he left, bolting the door after him.

Harold was even more confused now. And the balaclava, which had become the horror symbol of the age, brought back all of the fear that righteous anger had just displaced. He went back to the bucket in the corner.

At King's Cross station Maura had been waiting for almost half an hour at the platform gates. She had received another phone call that morning with further instructions which she had obeyed to the letter. She had also found Harold's car where they said it would be. Having searched it from top to bottom she failed to find a single clue about what had happened.

Commuters came and went, going about their business, sometimes brushing against her in their haste. The vaulted station reverberated to the sounds of railway engines and the public address system that bellowed into life at regular intervals. Her nerves had been hard at work on her and it was almost a relief when a solitary man seemed to materialise out of the rushing crowds. Even before he approached her she knew it was the man who had made the phone calls.

He wore jeans and a bomber jacket zipped up to the chin. He was younger than she had expected. Without saying anything he reached inside his jacket and showed her a photograph of Harold on his phone. She saw the fearful stare of her husband's eyes and began to cry. Patrick stood there until she managed to pull herself together.

"The passport," he said.

She nodded towards her handbag.

"Give it to me." He looked around to make sure there was no one paying them any special attention. "Quickly."

He opened it and glanced briefly through it.

"What do you … want it for? She blurted out. "He's a … dentist. There's no…"

"You'll be told later," he put the passport into an inside pocket. "If anyone asks where he is tell them he's gone to a conference. You understand?"

"Yes … but…"

"Now give me your phone please."

She asked why and he said that he needed it for security reasons. It would be returned to her later. When she handed it over he said, "Behave normally and nothing will happen to your husband. Now walk towards the platform gates."

She did as she was told. When she looked around he was gone, swallowed up by the crowds. She felt light on her feet, as if the ground had lost its solidity.

On the Underground she somehow expected that the group of West Indians sitting across from her would notice that something was wrong, but they didn't give her a second glance. In a trance-like state she picked up her car at the station car-park in Hertingfordbury and drove home. The house had never seemed so empty. Harold's recliner, magazine rack and standard lamp were like abandoned objects, mute testimony to his absence. She drew the curtains as if to keep the real world from intruding on her private nightmare which was just beginning.

The men examined the passport photograph under a naked light bulb and although nothing was said, the glances exchanged confirmed that Patrick would be the obvious choice for the mission. He would have to cut his hair and grey it a little. A contour product might be required for the nose while contact lenses and prosthetics for the jaws would also have to be considered. Horn-rimmed glasses and a greying moustache would complete the picture. The last two items had the considerable advantage of covering a large part of the face.

"Another damn moustache," he said resignedly.

"It won't be perfect," Paul admitted. "But it's the best we can do. At least visas won't be a problem. UK citizens don't need them."

"Are you sure?" Patrick asked.

"Yes, I'm sure. It's all part of the Wasp connection, the 'special' relationship."

The third man, who had been busy with a primus stove, emptied the contents of a tin into a bowl and brought it down to the cellar.

"You know this has to be done," Paul said.

"I know," Patrick replied. His commitment to the operation, did not, however, prevent him from regretting that a decent woman, like Maura, had to be involved.

"Just concentrate on the target. We've discussed it many times but if you have any questions or doubts now is the time to get them out of your system."

Patrick shrugged and then asked, "Is Dwyer really as influential as they say?"

"There's not much doubt about it. George says he'll stop at nothing and has more real power than the President. Anyway you've seen the reports. Our latest information shows that Kaltronics is preparing for massive expansion. And we know why, don't we?"

"Yes," Patrick said. He only needed Paul to confirm what he already knew. "There's no other way."

Paul nodded. "Remember your uncle in the 'sixties. He and all his compatriots believed in passive resistance. It came to nothing."

"Maybe it helped to end the Vietnam War earlier than…"

"No," Paul said adamantly. "The Americans knew they couldn't win short of nuclear escalation and they weren't prepared to go that far. Why? Because of fear of Soviet retaliation.

It would have been the first time in the history of warfare that the generals and the politicians would have destroyed themselves along with the cannon fodder. That was why the Cold War was actually good for peace. Neither side could risk an escalation. Now it's different. Since the Iraq War the Americans are fairly sure they can win any conventional war by superior technology. And the gap in technology is about to escalate beyond measure. Precision air strikes will take out the enemies' communication systems and without those, modern armies are crippled. So America won't even have to worry about casualties. No body bags. No bereaved parents crying on TV. The sky's the limit. The next stage will be the weaponisation of space. Dwyer is at the front edge of this too, and he has his stooge in place in Congress. It has to be done, Patrick. There's no alternative."

Patrick nodded slowly but another question formed in his mind. "Suppose someone else were to replace Dwyer…"

"Possible but not likely," Paul said. "He's a one-off and has personal control of well over one quarter of the US arms industry. Of course you're right to ask. We're dealing with probabilities. But even a fifty percent chance of world peace is worth … the effort. It will also send out a clear message that the real corporate power-brokers can no longer hide behind the politicians. They must be forced out of hiding."

"And worth the life of one man," Patrick said slowly. He'd read somewhere that President Truman didn't lose one hour's sleep over the bombing of Hiroshima and Nagasaki. The arithmetic was compelling: a hundred thousand lives to save an estimated half a million. If Hitler had been assassinated early in the war how many millions might have been saved? There were circumstances where the probabilistic ends justified the means. Patrick had only one more question.

"What if the dentist's wife refuses to travel?"

"And risk the life of her husband?" Paul queried. "I don't think so."

The third man returned from the cellar. "He's refusing to eat. Says he's dying from cold."

"Take him another blanket," Paul said. "He'll eat when he's hungry enough."

Later that evening Patrick peered through a crack in the floorboards. He saw Harold wearing the blanket as a shawl, picking at the stew which was stone cold. It was unlikely that anyone who knew Harold would be encountered in the States. Still, it was prudent to study his movements and mannerisms. And Patrick did just that until the light failed. Then he crawled into his sleeping bag and lay listening to the wind blowing through the broken windows and split timbers of the old farmhouse.

His brother, Jean, had worked for *Médecins sans Frontières* in Eastern Africa. He was a humanitarian and a specialist in tropical medicine. He had qualified from the Sorbonne just as Patrick was beginning his Engineering degree so they never spent much time together as students. Partly to make up for that Patrick spent the summers with him in Africa, making whatever contribution he could to hydrology projects. In that particular corner of the continent there were many tribal conflicts and that made the job of distributing food aid more difficult. The soldiers of the ruling junta took the food for themselves whenever they could, heedless of the extreme privation of their fellow countrymen, many of whom were barely surviving in primitive refugee camps.

The UN protective forces were less than useless and there weren't enough of them anyway, thanks to US indifference. Not one head of state of any Western country had bothered to visit the region where up to a million people had already died from starvation and related illnesses. It was a form of passive genocide. The country had no oil or other resources of interest to the West and that made all the difference.

On one occasion Jean had managed to get an unescorted Concern truck of food and medical supplies through to the refugee camp where he worked. He was almost as gaunt as the refugees themselves but his eyes were crystal clear, as if lit from within. A contingent of heavily armed troops bore down on the truck and pulled the driver out. They intended to take the provisions as well as the truck. Jean intervened, pleading with them. A corporal tried to push him aside. Jean stood in front of the truck and refused to be moved.

"Drive over him," the corporal shouted. The driver hesitated. A crowd began to form. Thin arms reached into the back of the truck trying to salvage what they could. Patrick saw a rifle butt descend on one of those arms, snapping it like a twig. Sick and afraid, he called to Jean to give it up; the odds were hopeless. But Jean stood his ground.

The corporal, armed with a Kaltronic assault weapon, came round to the front of the truck.

"You, fuck off. This is our property now."

"You don't need the food. They do." Jean swung his arm in the direction of the sprawling camp of open sewers and makeshift tents.

"White do-good bastard." The corporal levelled the machine gun. The bursts came fast in a barrage of continuous fire. Jean was virtually cut in two. About fifty rounds had ripped through him in five seconds. Dazed, Patrick rushed towards the body as if there might be something he could do.

"Drive over them," the corporal ordered as he jumped on the running board.

Patrick ducked out of the way just as the

wheels of the truck ground his brother's bloody form into the yellow earth. He blacked out …

He went back to Paris but couldn't concentrate on his studies. Besides, he was concerned about his mother, a widow, who never really came to terms with Jean's death and couldn't understand why his body hadn't been brought home to be buried in the family grave. Patrick couldn't bring himself to explain, though he did tell her that he had been laid to rest lovingly by many of the refugees who owed their lives to him. They had in fact done the best they could by erecting a cairn of stones over the blood-drenched site. Despite his best efforts, however, she could not recover her will to live and she slipped away eight months later on a May morning.

Patrick sold the house and wandered around Europe for the rest of that year, working at different jobs that couldn't hold his interest for very long. He hung around with the homeless and derelicts. In Rome he tried to prevent a prostitute from being beaten by her pimp and ended up with a stab wound in the shoulder and a broken jaw. She took him in and they lived together for a couple of months.

In London he worked mainly in hotels and often had occasion to overhear city gents discussing financial deals. The experience served to confirm his growing realisation that the wrong people were in jail. Tooth and claw capitalism was back in business after its total collapse in 2008. Eventually he decided it was time to stop drifting and he set about trying to get more meaningful jobs. He even tried to offer his services to the UN but, during the interview, he lost his temper.

"Why do you exist?" he asked.

The interviewer, a smooth-faced UN official, was taken aback by this turn of events and actually tried to answer the question.

"But you do nothing," Patrick followed up.

"We can't get involved in civil matters. Tribalism is a problem … We're not a paternalistic organisation. And we need the agreement of the US for most major decisions…"

"But then why do you exist? If you can't or won't do anything, why do you exist? What is your mission?"

"You don't understand," the bureaucrat said.

"It's not a difficult question," Patrick insisted, the phrase now repeating itself as if it had a life of its own. "Why do you exist?"

He didn't get the job.

In the years that followed, Patrick began to understand the power of the arms lobby around the world. Of course it was people who killed people, not guns. But putting powerful weapons into the hands of ill-trained violent men with fierce sectarian loyalties had to be a crime. Those Kaltronic assault weapons could fire a thousand rounds a minute. A few of them in the wrong hands could decimate an average town in less than half an hour. With their grenade attachments they could bring down aircraft flying at twenty thousand feet. One could only imagine what their large-scale weapons systems could do.

It was in Ankara that he met Paul and joined the Active Peace Force, a radical organisation that addressed itself to undermining the new destructive power structures that emerged after the ending of the Iraq war. Many members of the APF were Muslims, though not religious fundamentalists. It surprised him that so many members had French backgrounds, like Paul and himself. He had found his niche …

Now as he lay in the sleeping bag he could hear Harold snoring in the cellar beneath and he knew that the most important part of his life was about to begin.

CHAPTER 8

A COUPLE OF days later they brought a phone into the cellar and rehearsed Harold for a while before letting him talk to Maura. He told her that he was being treated reasonably well and that she should continue to follow instructions. It had by now become apparent to both of them how they were going to be used. Harold ended the brief conversation by referring to 'that bloody prize' as if he had foreseen all the dire consequences that would flow from it. That final note of rebuke before he was cut off reassured her in an odd way; it was the old Harold speaking.

Two days before the date of departure Patrick called to the house late in the evening. He had phoned earlier to make sure she would be alone and told her to leave the porch light off.

She confronted him in the living room. "You're not going to get away with this."

"With what?"

She didn't answer. She knew that something serious was planned, possibly assassination. "I'm not going to be an accomplice."

"To what?" he asked. "You don't know. Therefore you cannot be an accomplice."

She let it pass. There was another question she had to ask. "What if it … goes wrong.

Whatever it is. What will happen to Harold?"

"He will be freed whatever happens," Patrick said. "I give you my word."

"As a gentleman," she said with heavy sarcasm.

"As someone, who doesn't give his word without meaning it." He surveyed the room. "Take it or leave it."

She wasn't satisfied. "He can identify the kidnappers."

"No. We made sure of that. Has anyone asked about his whereabouts?"

"Some neighbours." For one crazy instant she was going to invite him to sit.

"And what did you tell them?"

"That he was at a conference."

"Good." He asked for her passport, tickets and invitations. He followed her upstairs and into the bedroom where she retrieved the items from a drawer of her dressing table. She handed them over, knowing that this was part of the ransom. It almost seemed like a civilised financial transaction. He spent some time studying the documents then placed them in an oilskin pouch which he wore like a shoulder holster inside his jacket. They were half-way down the stairs when the front door bell rang.

"Who is it?" he asked tersely.

"I don't know."

"Answer it and make some excuse. Get rid of them." He concealed himself in the cloakroom off the hall. She wondered if he was armed. In trepidation she opened the door. It was a woman representing the Simon community wondering if she had any old clothes for a jumble sale.

"I might … have," Maura said. "But … not now."

"That's OK," the woman said. "I'll be around again on Thursday." She left her a plastic sack for the clothes. "You could just leave this on the doorstep. Thank you very much."

"Not at all." Maura closed the door.

Patrick must have heard the conversation because he didn't challenge her. They stood in the unlit hall.

"You will go to Heathrow on Tuesday," he said.

"The flight is on Wednesday." She wondered why she bothered to put him right.

He nodded. "Yes, but on Tuesday you will check in to the airport hotel, the Trust House. You will spend the night there alone. Is that understood?"

"Yes." She presumed this was to foil any friends and neighbours who might be intending to give them a send-off.

"Then at 8.30 a.m. the next morning you take the hotel shuttle to the airport. You will wait at the British Airways desk. I will meet you there." He went over it again, slowly, step by step as if she were a child, and warned her that her movements would be closely watched.

He left shortly afterwards. She peered out a front window and saw him walk briskly into a light drizzle until he disappeared round the corner of the estate. If he had a car he had obviously left it some distance away.

Partly to keep occupied, she started to pack. Before the nightmare began she had hoped to buy some new outfits but there wasn't time for that now. In any case how could she do it in the circumstances? She would feel too guilty. She paused frequently, sometimes cried, then forced herself to continue. At about two in the morning she sat for a breather on the couch in the living room and fell asleep from nervous exhaustion.

Patrick did some packing too. Into a quite ordinary looking spectacle case he placed a pair of tinted glasses. The frames were hollow and contained a tiny syringe, no bigger than a sewing needle, and a phial of a lethal drug which had been developed by the KGB, a compound of parathion and hydrocyanic acid. If circumstances required some other method he would have to use his initiative. There were many variables and no guarantees.

The receptionist at the hotel looked hard at Maura as she checked in for the night. Even as she signed the registration card she was conscious of the girl's eyes on her. It wasn't her imagination or some delusion brought on by lack of sleep.

"I'm sorry," the girl said. "I seem to know you from somewhere. Did we meet …?"

"No, I don't think so," Maura said, going on tilt.

"Oh, wait now. I saw you on TV. You won that marvellous prize." She smiled broadly, glad to have solved the puzzle.

Maura's first instinct was to deny it but she recovered her composure in the nick of time. For some reason, however, she felt some explanation was in order. "I'm meeting my husband at the airport … tomorrow. He's been … away on business."

"I hope you have a wonderful time," the girl enthused.

"Thank you." Maura followed the porter into one of the elevators. He brought her to a room on the twelfth floor and deposited her bags on the luggage rack. He showed her how the central heating system and the TV worked and touched a finger to his forehead when she gave him a tip. The room was comfortable and bright, done out in Laura Ashley style. The windows, draped with enormously heavy curtains, looked towards the airport which, even at that distance, seemed to buzz with activity and brilliant light. She saw planes land and others take off; no doubt that would continue for most of the night; hence the heavy curtains – and triple glazing. The world never slept. Nor, according to some historian she'd heard on the radio, had there ever been one day when there was not a war being fought somewhere on the globe.

She unpacked only those items she needed for the night, leaving the big case where it was. She didn't open the suit bag but hung it up as it was, in the closet. The experience of spending one night alone in a hotel room was new to her and she felt lonely and miserable. Of course the circumstances that had brought her here were hardly normal.

She wasted as much time in the bath as she could. Then, wrapping herself in the deep-piled towels she sat in front of the TV for a while, but it failed to distract her in any way or give any respite from her predicament. She put on her night-dress and lay on top of the bed. The room was stifling; she got up to turn down the thermostat but it made no perceptible difference. Because of the air-conditioning system the windows were hermetically sealed so there was no way of letting a little cold air in. Finally, she turned off the thermostat altogether, again to no effect. It was either broken or it served only a cosmetic purpose. By this stage she was too tired to sleep and she tossed and turned on the counterpane all night listening to the changing pitch of aircraft as they taxied, took-off and landed.

At about 6 in the morning she had a cold shower to try to perk herself up. She repacked the few loose items and rang for a porter to bring down her cases. In the fairly empty dining room she had two cups of black coffee and managed most of a croissant. Then she paid her bill and waited outside the main entrance for the hotel shuttle bus. It was bitterly cold; she almost wished to be back in that stifling room again.

The minibus dropped her at the British Airways terminal where she loaded her cases on to a trolley and went through the electronic doors. She arrived at the check-in desk well before eight. Patrick joined her almost immediately; he may have been there even earlier. He looked surprisingly like Harold, bespectacled, grey at the temples. The moustache, however, was a little too full and dark. He didn't greet her as such but he did look closely at her and asked if she was feeling all right.

"Why?" she inquired coldly.

"You look a little … tired."

"Is it any wonder?" she snarled. Had he no awareness of what he had put her through? The cheek of the bastard!

He seemed tense as the ground hostess checked them in and arranged seat numbers. He accepted the boarding cards and kept his eyes on her as she checked the passports. She returned them with a smile.

"Have a good flight, Mr. and Mrs. Crowther. And do make use of the BA lounge.

Just show your boarding passes to the receptionist."

But first they had to pass the gauntlet of security – a humiliating ritual designed by the US to keep everyone in fear of terrorism. Patrick got through relatively unscathed because he had immediately handed over his toiletries in a special plastic bag. The spectacle case was opened, the contents glanced at; then it was handed back. Maura, on the other hand set off the metal detector and had to stand in a Christ-like posture while she was being frisked, both manually and electronically.

Her mood improved a little in the magnificently appointed lounge. She had another cup of coffee while Patrick flicked through some business magazines. The occupants were nearly all men; some were making phone calls, others texting or sending faxes. There were several intense individuals using laptop computers. Apart from herself and the fawning hostesses, there were only two other women in the lounge and they were immaculately dressed and groomed. The younger one was almost certainly a supermodel, although Maura couldn't quite place her. She felt dowdy by comparison but didn't worry unduly about it. This was not her normal scene, nor had she any expectation that it would become so. No, she simply wanted to savour it once – though not under present circumstances.

On closer inspection she recognised, from TV, a politician and two senior churchmen. No doubt all of the people in the room were highly successful in their own fields but some had a higher profile than others. None of those whom she categorised as tycoons had ever, to her knowledge, appeared on TV or been written about in the papers. They probably spent fortunes to maintain their privacy. Some of the real power elite were doubtless in this very room but could not be recognised by the ordinary citizen. It was a vaguely worrying thought. Still, it didn't preoccupy her for very long as she explored the facilities on offer. She went to the Ladies and tested different perfumes on her wrist. She would have liked to try the Jacuzzi but there wasn't enough time.

She was almost disappointed when the flight was called, but there were more treats in store. On boarding the aircraft and turning left towards the club-class section, she was given a posy of orchids. As soon as they were seated they were offered champagne or bucks fizz. So was everyone else. She was glad not to be singled out and fussed over as a 'prize-winner'. It would have been like entering a top school as a scholarship girl – bright but not really up to par socially.

Even Patrick seemed to be impressed when the powerful craft charged down the runway and hurtled into the air, veering out over the Atlantic with a surging sense of freedom and adventure. Sipping a second glass of champagne, Maura put on her headphones and listened to one of the excellent music programmes. No wonder these business men who were already pecking away at laptops developed power complexes. This was high speed, high tech, high life, high everything. Poor Harold! How he would have enjoyed this. With a start she remembered that he had turned it all down long before the kidnapping.

Patrick began to unwind; nothing much could happen on a flight. He seemed more relaxed, not that it made any difference to her. Christ, she was so confused, guilt, fear and enjoyment coming at her in waves, each cancelling the other but only for a while.

The meal began with beluga and Finnish vodka: this was followed by glazed salmon, and medallions of veal, all courses accompanied by judiciously chosen wines. There was even a dessert wine with the baked Alaska, then vintage port with the cheese board, followed by twenty-year-old Cognac. It was also the first nourishing meal that Maura had eaten in over a week.

When she looked out the porthole she could see clouds going past and there was an exhilarating sense of speed which made her feel giddy, though no doubt that was also caused by the wine. At one point she thought she saw Patrick smiling at her. She sobered up quickly and selected one of the in-flight movies.

Somewhere in mid-Atlantic reality intruded. Here she was enjoying her flight, her prize, while her husband's life lay in the balance and she was being used by a would-be killer. Life had played some strange tricks on her but nothing like this. The top of her skull began to lift. Had she done the right thing by not going to the police? Had she really any choice in the matter?

She went to the lavatory and threw up. She made some running repairs to her face and returned to her seat as if nothing had happened. She fell into a deep sleep and when she awoke she realised with embarrassment that her head had slumped onto Patrick's shoulder.

Accompanied by a teacher colleague, Barbara Woodside, Maura's bridge partner, rang the bell of the Crowther's front door at the southern end of Hertingfordbury.

"That's strange," she said. "The house looks empty. But they're not going until tomorrow. Wednesday. I'm sure it's Wednesday."

"Maybe Harold got back early from his conference," the other woman said. "Maybe they decided to leave a day earlier than planned."

"I suppose that's possible," Barbara said uncertainly. She peered through a crack in the venetian blinds of the sitting room window and then went around the side of the house until she had a view of the back garden. "But whatever about Harold it's just not like Maura to disappear without a word to anyone. We had that little 'do' arranged and everything."

"But Maura wouldn't have known that," the other woman pointed out reasonably.

"Still…" Barbara wasn't satisfied.

Later that afternoon when the pupils were hard at work solving for x and y, she called the surgery from her classroom, and was surprised to learn that Harold and Maura had taken leave a little earlier than intended, and that a locum had been employed by his junior partner.

Barbara, a Benjamin Black aficionado, ruminated on this when the school-day ended, and unburdened herself to her husband over tea that evening. He was eating some of the sandwiches and canapés that had been prepared for the Crowther send-off; there was no point in wasting them.

"What's odd?" he inquired between mouthfuls.

With infinite patience she again explained the situation to him and waited for his verdict.

"I suppose it's a bit strange all right," he conceded. "Still, there could be several different explanations."

"Like what?"

"Oh, anything could have happened." He waved an airy hand, then lowered it to spear a cocktail sausage. Either he hadn't been listening or he couldn't come up with a plausible hypothesis.

"Hmmm." Barbara sat down. She would have to puzzle it out for herself. Why would they have left earlier than expected without a word to any of the neighbours? Was it possible that they leading some sort of double life? The very thought made her want to laugh; but she couldn't quite dismiss it because in the world of crime- writing there were always surprises. Nothing could be taken at face value; black swans abounded. Was it her imagination or had Maura been behaving a little oddly in the past week – even on that occasion when they met in the supermarket? It bore thinking about.

CHAPTER 9

PATRICK TENSED UP again as they entered the concourse of Kennedy Airport which was bedecked with Christmas decorations. He made Maura link her arm through his and gave her the passports to present at immigration. This would be the first real test. They shuffled forward in the queue which moved at a snail's pace. Gone were the comforts of Club-class and the sense of privilege; they were now busted to the ranks of ordinary passengers and subjected to the same bureaucratic procedures. They edged their way towards the yellow line. When eventually it was their turn Maura tendered the passports to the immigration officer with a rather forced smile. He entered the numbers into a computer. Then he looked from them to the passport photos and back again. Patrick stood absolutely still. He was worried about the biometric security data encoded in the passport. Paul had arranged for an experienced hacker to use a 'backdoor' to alter the data; Patrick could only hope that it had been done properly.

"Christmas in New York," Maura said with what she hoped was a wistful sigh.

"Visiting?" the officer inquired, staring hard at them over his half glasses.

"Yes," Maura said. "A dream come true."

"You'll be here for New Year's?"

"Absolutely. In Washington. Where better to see in the New Year?" Her enthusiasm rang false but why was she even making the effort?

The officer had one final look at the passports and then at his computer- screen.

"Enjoy," he said, nodding them through with a smile. Patrick got a sky cap to take the bags off the carousel. Clearing customs was little more than a formality. A custom's officer opened one of Maura's bags, rummaged through some clothes and toiletries and that was that.

"Thanks," Patrick said.

"For what?"

"Back there." He jerked his head to indicate the immigration area.

"Let's get one thing straight," she said. "I have to go along with this. You're holding my husband hostage."

When they got to the arrivals area she noticed a courier holding aloft a sign which read, "Mr. and Mrs. Crowther". They went towards him, a beaming young African-American who welcomed them warmly, gave instructions to the sky cap and ushered them through the crowds into a waiting limousine.

"Art's the name," he said. "I work for the TV Network, KNYBS. We've got everything laid on for you at the hotel. Many of the other prize-winners have already arrived. There's a reception for you all this evening and you'll have plenty of time to freshen up before that.

I'm staying at the hotel too so if there's anything you need just holler."

"Thank you," Maura said.

Art drove fast and skillfully, not even slowing at the toll plazas which read the electronic disk on his windscreen. Maura could hardly wait to see the Manhattan skyline and when it came into view she was not disappointed. She was able to pick out the most famous skyscrapers, the UN, Chrysler, Empire State. With a shudder she noticed the building that had replaced the twin towers. The bridges, though old-fashioned and rather brutish in structure, had a stamp of character that couldn't be ignored. The city itself. though massive in scale, had a lived-in feel and was fairly run-down in places. They passed wire-fenced parks and squares where kids played basketball and softball. Roller-bladers and bicycle couriers wove in and out between the cars, heedless of risk. It was like a perpetual-motion machine and she knew at once why it was called the 'city that never sleeps'.

"New York," Maura sighed under her breath. If only her dream had not been hijacked and turned upside-down.

Occasionally Art struck his forehead with the heel of his hand at the ineptitude of other drivers. At other times he would raise his hands and let them fall helplessly back on the steering wheel. This was a city, Maura thought, where you were expected to express yourself loudly to have any chance of being heard above the surrounding din and ever-present distractions.

At the hotel they were greeted by one of the managers and escorted to their suite. This was like the British Airways lounge all over again. There were fresh flowers in the bedroom and champagne on ice in the sitting room. Art and the manager both left their cards, promising to be at their beck and call.

After an awkward silence Patrick said, "I'll sleep here." He put his bag on the sofa, opened it and removed the spectacle case which he placed in an inside pocket. "You probably want to … I'll leave you alone for a while." He left the room and went down to the lobby.

Maura showered, quickly – in case he might return – and put on a simple dress. She looked out at the city. As evening drew in the lights began to come on, millions of lights, many of them reflected in the Hudson. She could have stayed there for hours watching this amazing transformation.

When Patrick returned he asked if she were ready.

"For what?"

"The reception."

"I don't want to go to that," she said.

"We have to attend," he insisted. "Everything must appear normal."

They found themselves in a large function room on the third floor where Art introduced them to many of the other guests. These were not the celebrities they would be rubbing shoulders with on New Year's Eve, but people like themselves who had won the same prize in their own countries.

"I don't think there are any other British folk here," Art said, "though there are a lot of Europeans. Here for instance." He introduced them to Tim and Clare O'Malley, an Irish couple, and excused himself to greet some other guests.

"I was born to this," Clare O'Malley said with a grin. She stopped a passing waiter and invited Maura and Patrick to help themselves to champagne.

"I know what you mean," Maura said. "We were all born to it. Everyone should be pampered like this at least once in their lives." She relished the opportunity of having someone to chat to at last, a normal person.

"It's like Warhol's thing about fifteen minutes of fame," Clare said.

"I know what you mean. It's such a change to have meals served up; no need to lift a finger."

"Yeah, we're being lifted and laid, all right," Tim offered.

"I wonder," Clare mused, "whether you could become blasé about it. I mean, the mistresses of the big houses in the nineteenth century must've taken it all for granted. They probably didn't even realize how privileged they were."

"Right," Maura said. "And what did a holiday mean to them? Probably nothing because they were so used to being waited on anyway. And they also had to worry about what the servants were up to in their absence."

"Port out, starboard home," Clare said. "But you're right. You can have too much of a good thing. Still, once in a while doesn't hurt. Just look at that spread." She gestured towards the nearest buffet table, which had a remarkable variety of hot and cold food, dishes and savouries drawn from different national cuisines. In the middle of the table, stood an ice sculpture of *Old Father Time*, slowly melting. Pointing this out, Clare said, "We were told that he'll collapse into a pool of water at the stroke of midnight on New Year's Eve."

"We'll be in Washington then," Maura said. She was vaguely conscious of Patrick's eyes on her. Was he checking to see if she was playing her part, or did it indicate something else?

"I'm really looking forward to that. We'll get to mingle with the great and the good."

The two men were slower to strike up a rapport but eventually Tim said, "If you want a real drink there's a good malt over there on the bar."

"Malt?" Patrick seemed puzzled.

"A single malt," Tim explained. "Not bad for Scotch."

"Oh right. Thanks. I'll stick with the wine."

"Have you been to the States before?"

"Once," Patrick said. "For a short visit. You?"

"I worked here for a few years as a student. Boston and Baltimore. Great country."

"Yes it is." It pained Patrick to agree, but now was not the time to reveal his true views.

"And there are something like thirty million Irish-Americans, so we kind of feel at home over here. Of course, so do you – the WASP connection."

"The WASP...? Oh yes, very true."

Tim studied the level in his glass. "If it's necessary for one country to hold the balance of power I'm glad it's the US."

"Why is that?" Patrick asked

"Who else could you trust? Germany? Japan? Britain? Look at their record for war and domination. No, if we need a Globocop, I'm glad it's the good old US of A. Some mistakes, yes, like Iraq for example. But there's a basic decency here and none of the trappings of empire."

"Maybe," Patrick said carefully, "the US is changing, becoming more like the old war-mongers?"

"God, let's hope not." Tim plucked another drink from a passing tray and replaced the empty glass

Maura and Clare excused themselves and went to the Ladies together as if they were bosom pals from way back.

"Your husband is a quiet man," Clare

remarked. "Deep, I'd say. Still waters. Handsome too."

"Handsome…? I suppose so." Maura was brought down to earth again. She thought of Harold, the last photo she'd seen, his startled expression. But there was something about the background … what was it? God, it looked like a cellar. He was underground. She shuddered.

"It was Tim who won the quiz," Clare said. "I never thought I'd get to visit the States again. When I was training to be a hotel manager I spent some time in a modest boutique hotel in Boston. It was good experience… And I've some cousins in Philadelphia though we're not that close." She frizzed her hair in front of the mirror with the handle of her comb. "We've only been here a few days and already our minds have been broadened, as they say. And you see so many different racial groups in the streets. We thought we were multicultural, back home in Ireland. But we're not even in the same league."

"Maybe you're better off in the long run," Maura said without thinking. On reflection, she wondered if she wasn't just parroting Harold, who sometimes worried aloud about the fact that ultimately all Britons would become brown-skinned – and to avoid such an outcome had gladly voted for Brexit. She had gone the other way, thus cancelling out his vote, but she hadn't told him. This recollection made her feel disloyal.

"Hey, Harold is a dentist," Tim announced when they returned. Patrick had obviously loosened up a bit, and it was clear to Maura that he had stolen all her husband's plumes, including his profession. Nevertheless, he looked a little ill at ease.

"I had a wisdom tooth extracted a few years back..." Clare began. And there followed an intense series of dental anecdotes, one more lurid than the next. It was obvious that the O'Malleys were fond of story-telling and were unlikely to pester Patrick for scientific explanations. Sensing this, he joined in the laughter, showing his own rather large and strong teeth.

Clare introduced a German couple to the Crowther's.

"We have to be careful now," Tim joked lamely. "The Germans are the paymasters of the EU."

The German couple made disparaging noises and wondered aloud if they might have to fill the hole left by Britain. They asked the Crowther's whether there was any chance that Britain might re-join the EU. Maura fielded the question.

"I don't think so," she said. "Our government really believes that the EU was damaging to our interests. I personally voted to remain."

The German couple wondered if there should not be a second referendum and they again looked to Maura for a response.

"Well, I would like to see that happen," she said. "But the government would probably think it would come across as a flip-flop… You know how in politics a change of direction is often perceived as a sign of weakness."

"I think the British government has some unreal expectations," Tim put in. "I mean some of them think that Britain can regain its former, imperial glory. But that ship has sailed, hasn't it?"

Maura began to formulate a reply when they were distracted by a speech of welcome, just started by an executive of KNYBS, the TV network that had sponsored the prizes. She sketched out the programme for the next seven days, terminating in Washington. She stressed that all of the shows, trips, concerts were entirely optional. People could do as they pleased, though she hoped they would all turn up for the main New Year's Eve event in Washington DC because it promised to be a spectacular affair.

The O'Malleys left shortly after the speech ended to take in a Broadway show they'd already booked for.

"Would you like to go to a show? Patrick inquired after they'd left.

Maybe it was the champagne, or the surroundings, but Maura couldn't help laughing. Was this kidnapper / assassin actually trying to give her a good time?

"Are you mad?"

"We might as well do something." He seemed less uptight; maybe some minute particle of the carnival mood had gotten to him. As if realising this, he added "We must behave normally."

They finally compromised on a movie and a Thai meal afterwards. Maura asked so many questions of the waiter about spices and sauces that he eventually brought out the chef who for some reason appeared quite defensive and quickly disappeared back into the kitchen without having revealed very much about his culinary arts.

As they walked back to the hotel they passed a corner of Central Park. She pictured Patrick and herself going for a ride in one of the horse-drawn carriages. It beggared belief; the mind was capable of extraordinary ironies. Light snow swirled around them but melted almost as soon as it touched the pavement. She still had a child's way of assessing snowfalls: would there be enough to make a snowman? Would it be of the right powdery consistency? The answer in this instance was in the negative. A pity. There was something about a good solid fall of snow that had always appealed to her, a startling change that seemed to promise something entirely new and fresh. Of course it never lasted. In time the thaw would come and bring with it the awful muddy slush that always seemed to find a way of seeping inside the stoutest shoes. But for a while, as long as the snow stayed pristine on the ground, there was hope everywhere.

She went to bed as soon as they went to the suite. Patrick stayed in the sitting room for a while and then slept on the sofa. Through the partition she could hear him breathing, evenly and without snores or sudden throat-clearings. It was an unaccustomed sound.

The next morning she went into the small kitchen to make coffee, forgetting all about room service. She couldn't very well bring Patrick a cup but she did knock on the door to say there was coffee made. There was no response. She pushed the door open and looked in. There was evidence that he had slept on the couch but he was definitely not there at that moment.

She consulted her watch. Seven-thirty. Strange. But none of her concern. The fact that she did not have to worry about his movements was disorienting in itself. She sat down with her coffee at the window and watched the city ratchet itself up into a higher gear.

He turned up about half an hour later in running kit, having been out in Central Park jogging around the reservoir with all the other like-minded fitness fanatics.

"I always wanted to…" He pointed to the bathroom. "Do you mind if I…"

"Of course." She waved him towards the door. This politeness was bizarre and she felt a complete idiot. The social conventions for this situation had not yet been invented and probably never would be. "I'm going shopping this morning." It was a statement but in a way she was asking his permission. She didn't quite catch his reply, which was distorted by the acoustics of the bathroom, but she thought it was, "Buy me a present." No, it couldn't have been that; her ears were deceiving her. But he did seem to trust her more now. And why not? If she'd come this far without jeopardising his precious mission, whatever it was, he'd have to conclude she'd go the whole way. Yes, she was paying the ransom in instalments, hour by hour, and he had no complaints so far. By now she was disposed to believe that if she played her part, they would not hurt Harold. But there was likely to be another victim or victims, and in that regard she had no idea whether or not she was doing the right thing.

Although 9/11 had happened over twenty years ago, it had not faded from memory. The terrorist threat was still very real, and former Presidents, even Barack Obama, had continued to instill fear into the American public. Maura didn't think Patrick was a terrorist as such – in a way he seemed too boyish – but she couldn't be sure. How much damage was he planning to do? It had to be significant, given the time and planning that went into the kidnapping of Harold.

The shopping expedition wasn't exactly a spree; her heart wasn't in it. But she did every floor by rote in Macey's, bewildered by the extraordinary range of goods and services on offer. In a way she was establishing her independence by going out on her own. Despite the enormous size of the store it was congested with Christmas shoppers who went about their business with grim determination, sometimes elbowing her out of their way. In the Ladies Department she looked at some dresses but couldn't quite summon the energy to try them on. She bought a magazine to give herself a countenance in a coffee shop where she had a light snack.

After that she got something of a second wind and bought several ties for Harold. They were a little modern and colourful but maybe he would like them. For some reason she assumed that after his ordeal he would become a little more adventurous.

Outside, it was slightly overcast, a grey day with a distant wintry sun doing its best to come out. Her prediction of the previous night was correct: the snow hadn't lasted. She tried a couple of times to hail a cab but without success; she couldn't quite summon the forcefulness to step into the street and make eye contact with the drivers. Only New Yorkers could carry that off properly. It didn't matter much. She consulted a pocket map she'd acquired in the absence of her cell, and set out walking.

When she got back to the hotel suite, Patrick was on the phone. She put her ear to the adjoining door, which he hadn't quite closed. Her French was good enough to make out the gist of the conversation.

"…so things have gone all right … so far. What was that? No … no problem there … You're sure Dwyer will be there … on the night? Good … Yes, I think it will be necessary … Hold on for a second, Paul…"

Although Maura caught the final words she didn't realise their import until Patrick drew apart the sliding doors and confronted her.

"Do you always eavesdrop?"

"Only when my husband's been kidnapped," she retorted sharply.

He took her by the hand and led her to the phone.

"Put Mr. Crowther on." To her he said, "Talk to him. One minute."

She took the receiver and cupped it with her hand as if she could achieve some degree of privacy.

"Harold, darling … How are you?"

"All right … You?" His voice sounded faint. She hoped it was because of a bad connection.

"Fine. I'm fine. You must be feeling so …

Don't worry. Everything will be all right…"
With her free hand she wiped her eyes.

"So you went on that trip?" His voice didn't sound quite so distant.

"I had to, Harold."

"Had to?"

The note of rebuke struck at her senses. Maybe they hadn't told him the whole plan. Maybe he thought she had gone on a skite while he was imprisoned by a group of terrorists or whatever they were.

"Harold … you might not have the full picture…"

"I think I do. And I think there were other ways…"

"Please listen. I have to do this … It's part of the ransom…"

"Enough!" Paul's voice cut in roughly. Patrick took the receiver from her. She left the room in distress and threw herself on the bed. Did Harold not understand that she had no choice? She began to doubt herself and her own motives. His rebuke, delivered from four thousand miles away, continued to drill into her mind. The only thing she had to hold on to was the fact that Harold was all right; if dignity was still his main concern then it was unlikely that he was in fear for his life. That thought helped in recovering her composure. But it was quickly replaced by a more difficult concern: What of the neighbours? Would they simply assume that she and Harold had left for the airport early or would they come to some other conclusion and if so, would they act on it? She had no way of knowing, although she had a feeling that her bridge partner, Barbara Woodside, for one, would be reluctant to set aside her natural curiosity, and she could, without realising it, place Harold in jeopardy.

The hotel organised a number of tours for the afternoon. One would take in the main museums and art galleries, the Metropolitan, MOMA, and the Guggenheim. This was the one that Patrick suggested but Maura demurred, preferring the alternative which was a sight-seeing tour of Manhattan.

"We have to stay together for appearances sake," Patrick pointed out as they went down in the elevator.

"Well, I'm not going to museums," Maura gave no quarter. She knew that she hadn't much to bargain with and realised full well that she was also a hostage in a very real sense. However, she was determined to exploit whatever scope she had. Before they reached the ground floor she reckoned that Patrick was about to give in, but as it happened he didn't have to because they ran into the O'Malleys in the lobby and they were involved in the same wrangle.

"Ah, Maura, the very woman," Clare greeted her. "You and me. Sightseeing, right. Leave the museums to the fuddy-duddies. Come on, girl."

Tim and Patrick exchanged helpless glances.

"You'll miss Van Gogh's Irises," Tim said with his last throw of the dice.

"I have plenty of irises in the garden at home," Clare threw back with a laugh. She linked Maura by the arm. "He couldn't tell the difference between an iris and a dandelion." Before disappearing into the revolving doors she delivered her parting shot. "Enjoy the museums, you pseudo-intellectuals."

The bus, a double-decker, headed south through Broadway. The two women at first tried the upper open deck but it was too cold and they went downstairs where they seated themselves at the back. The courier pointed out the sights to them, including Times Square, where preparations were already being made for a huge public celebration for New Year's Eve. They passed through the garment district, Soho, the Village, and Chinatown, then looped back for a while to see the ritzy shopping areas along Fifth Avenue. Maura was intrigued by how elegant modern architecture could be, especially when enough space was allowed for plazas and parks to soften and humanise the massive buildings, many of which, she observed, had roof gardens. She was also struck by the number of homeless people who pushed shopping carts full of old cloths and bedding around those same high-rent spaces.

"How do they survive?" she wondered

aloud.

"I don't know," Clare said. "I think they sleep in the subway or near steam vents. But that's capitalism for you. I read somewhere that two percent of Americans own ninety percent of the wealth. No wonder the rich run the country."

When they got near Battery Park there was a choice: a walking tour of Wall Street or a boat trip to the Statute of Liberty and Ellis Island. The courier advised them that, because of the cold, the latter was not for the faint-hearted.

"We're not faint-hearted, are we?" Clare asked.

"Absolutely not," Maura concurred.

The boat journey out wasn't too bad. For a while they actually stayed on deck watching the waves scroll over the bow. The Statute of Liberty got bigger and bigger as they approached and they could hardly believe the dimensions as they finally stood at the bottom looking up at the people who moved around the viewing platform inside the torch. Clare confessed to a fear of enclosed spaces so they didn't go inside the statute.

The main building at Ellis Island was less impressive as a structure but it had a resonance that moved her deeply. Clare said that she could almost hear echoes of sick and desperate voices, pleading to be allowed into the New World. Both of them ignored the courier's facts and figures; they seemed irrelevant somehow.

The return boat trip was not very pleasant. Dusk had fallen and a chill sleet-bearing wind made the water choppy. They stayed below deck, their coats and scarves wrapped tightly about them.

"Talk about your huddled masses," Clare said, her teeth chattering.

"I could kill for a brandy," Maura groaned. She actually felt a little sea sick.

They were glad to get back on the bus. The driver had considerately kept the engine and heating system going. They started to glow in the warmth as the bus headed back towards the hotel.

They made a foursome for dinner and then went with several of the other guests to a comedy store, Catch a Rising Star, where amateur stand-up comics tried out between the professional acts. As they were settling into their seats Clare spoke for them all when she announced that she was determined to last the pace even if it killed her.

It was a terrific show and Maura laughed so loudly at one point that the emcee singled her out for a few well-directed taunts. A couple of the younger comics 'died' and the New York crowd, far from being sympathetic, tried to hasten their demise by heckling. "Never give a sucker an even break', seemed to be the motto. Excluding the foreigners, it was a tough room and Maura realised the truth of the Ethel Merman line, "If you can make it here you can make it anywhere". The emcee did, however, come out to rescue the casualties as soon as they went into a downward spiral. Once when he led a youngster off the stage, Maura said, "It's not fair. They didn't give him a chance."

"He'll be back though," Clare suggested. "He just needs more attack, more confidence. They're like lion-tamers. We're the lions. They mustn't let us smell their fear."

"And he stank to high heaven," Tim remarked.

Patrick was silent for the most part and it wasn't until they got back to the hotel that the reason emerged.

"Did you really find it so amusing?" he asked her.

"Yes." She felt like calling him a stick-in the mud.

"Some of the jokes were racist."

"They had a go at everyone," she pointed out. "There was that gag about white trash. It's satire."

"Satire should be directed against the powerful," he said, "not against the poor and the minorities. Some of the jokes were sick, the products of a sick society."

"There was some black humour," she conceded. "But it was meant to be taken with a grain of salt."

"You might take it that way but there are a lot of ordinary people who would be influenced by it."

She gave him a sidelong glance, intrigued by what he'd said. "I'm an ordinary person." She immediately regretted personalising it.

"No, I don't think so." He gave a wan smile. "This situation must be hard on you. I realise that. But you cope well with it. I think it takes courage … moral courage."

"I'm not the one with the bad conscience," she replied a little too glibly.

"I don't have a bad conscience." The down lights of the hotel lobby threw his face into shadow, making it appear even more gaunt and intense.

"Look," she said earnestly. "Give it up. Whatever it is, don't do it. Just walk away." She felt like an older sister counselling a wild sibling to save him from himself. The truth began to dawn on her; she didn't want him to come to harm even though he had treated her and Harold so abominably. She had the impression that he was in over his head. On the other hand, this could be pure rationalization on her part. It bothered her that she had no clear line on him.

"I don't think you understand what's involved," he said grimly.

"Maybe I understand more than you think."

He looked at her as if this might just possibly be true.

CHAPTER 10

THE DAYS TO the end of the year were being counted down. The TV screens were filled nightly with retrospective programmes about the year that was drawing to a close.

The Christmas tree outside the Ralston home had been switched on. Evelyn could see it from her bedroom window. It was a graceful spruce with white fairy lights, much more elegant than the other multi-coloured ones that mushroomed on the well-manicured lawns of Bethesda. Stanley was beginning to wind down for the Christmas period. His Congressional Committee held their last meeting of the year in the Capitol. The back-slapping banter of the members was at odds with the decision they had just reached.

Much to Evelyn's relief, William, the Deputy Chairman of CASA, had been persuaded to take a holiday. She was never really sure whether he was paranoid or simply a workaholic but, for some odd reason, he seemed to view her as a rival for Stanley's ear. In one way it was pathetic; in another it was frightening. At any rate she was glad he had disappeared for a few days. She was also glad about something else. Stanley and she were going to their holiday home in West Virginia for Christmas but he was going to go back there for

New Year's Eve. She didn't ask why. The important thing was that this would leave her free to attend the ball in DC on her own and spend some time with Lawrence.

Shortly after Stanley got back from the Capitol he got a call from Lawrence, who asked how the last meeting of his committee had gone.

"A diplomatic minuet," Stanley said. "Nothing substantive." The long fingers of his free hand played a riff on the desktop.

"I'll be in DC after Christmas," Lawrence said. "We can go into more detail then." He wondered if Stanley was keeping something from him. His greatest concern was that the military might go cold on the 'big project' underway in Kaltronics, but there was no evidence of that; in fact the opposite, if his contacts in the Pentagon were to be believed. It was better not to discuss it even though they were on a secure line.

"Sure." Stanley emitted a light laugh. He knew there was something else on the agenda, and he was right.

Lawrence told him of an arms deal which was in the offing with an East European country. "I've cleared it with State and the Pentagon, and there's no problem with intellectual property rights …"

"Well, it sounds as if you've gone through the right channels." Stanley pressed the hands-free button and leant back in his chair, interlocking his fingers behind his head.

"The question is, can they pay in hard currency?"

"You're covered by export credit insurance, I take it…"

"That's not the point, Stanley. Are they in funds? Dollar funds?"

So that was it. "The first tranche of US aid was disbursed last week."

"I know that, but State was coy about the amount." Lawrence wondered why he had to make all the running; it was like pulling teeth. "The order comes to 780 million dollars. One hundred of that is in the form of counter-trade. Another hundred gives Kaltronics an option on mineral rights. That leaves 580 million hard cash. Are they good for that?"

"In principle, yes."

"Meaning?"

"The aid tranche was well in excess of that, but it was earmarked for education and rural development."

"Earmarked or tied?"

"Not tied, no."

"OK." Lawrence was satisfied at last. Money was fungible. If the recipient country preferred arms, then education and rural development could wait. It was their decision, based on their priorities. The boys and girls at US Aid mightn't like it but they would continue to draw their pay.

"We're starting to plan for our next term." It

was Stanley's turn to name a price.

"Good, the sooner the better," Lawrence said, ignoring the effete use of the plural. "I've been doing some thinking about that. I can put our PR people on to it. The polls aren't so hot at the moment, as you know. But a good, targeted campaign can turn that around."

"Polls don't mean that much," Stanley said.

"They can be misleading at times," Lawrence conceded. "But it wouldn't do to be overconfident. I hear the Democrats are getting behind a strong candidate."

"Stevenson?"

"Yes."

"He's a rube."

"A little rough around the edges, I grant you. But that can easily be fixed by the handlers. And look at his record. He was a shoo-in for Governor. He's saying all the right things about healthcare out here. Remember, we've got an ageing population, and other demographics are on his side…"

"He's a populist."

"Yes. But that means votes. And he's clean, pristine…"

"Ha. No one is." Stanley leant further back in his chair and put his feet on the desk. Lawrence's condescending tone was getting to him, but he had no intention of revealing that.

"Maybe, maybe not. It would require a lot of digging in any case. And muck-raking can go both ways."

The conversation became desultory after that and they signed off a few minutes later. Stanley was irritated. Who the hell did Dwyer think he was? He had never really liked him; the man had no finesse and had no respect for political office. The sense of victory Stanley once had by taking Evelyn away from him had sustained him for many years, but now it was beginning to wear thin.

At dinner that night he mentioned that he'd been talking to Lawrence.

"About what?" Evelyn asked casually.

"Oh, just some items of business."

"I see." She had no intention of showing too much interest. If Stanley wanted to enlarge on it that was up to him. She was not going to plead for information at her own table.

After a short silence Stanley said, "The man is conducting arms sales in the holiday period. He just can't let up." He gave a slight shudder of distaste which amused Evelyn, who was almost tempted to say that some people had to work for a living and that new money was just as good as old money, not that Stanley had much of the latter. Instead, she decided to follow the line of inquiry put to her by Lillian.

"After all the SALT negotiations we're still no further along." She contemplated a fat prawn hanging from the end of her fork.

"Those negotiations were about nuclear arms," he said, stating the obvious.

"Does it really make much difference?" she

followed up. "Aren't conventional weapons so powerful now as to be almost as destructive?"

"More targeted," he corrected her. "More precise." The fastidious way he spoke seemed to underscore the point.

"Exactly. They allow the aggressor to win without any losses. They make war too easy for the high-tech countries."

"So?" He dabbed the corner of his mouth with a linen napkin and gave her a curious glance.

"A country like ours with a high-tech advantage should use it responsibly…"

"Which we do."

"Do we?"

"Yes." He signalled to the butler that they were ready for coffee. "Our role in the world is a very complex matter."

She ignored the patronising note. "Shouldn't we lead by example? For starters, we could abandon the idea of pre-emptive defence…" She pressed on for a while, though the conversation was becoming tiresome.

"We do lead by example. That is our main policy." He stirred his coffee.

From long experience she knew that the word 'policy' was a smoke screen. Even store clerks used it as in, 'It's not our policy to give credit'. Evelyn wasn't all that surprised. She never really believed her views counted for much with Stanley or his colleagues, least of all William, who for some strange reason seemed to overestimate her influence and tried to keep her out of 'policy' discussions.

Stanley might, however, have done her the courtesy of hearing her out, but he didn't and that was that. She felt voiceless even though she was right at the hub of things. What must it be like for the tens of millions out there who were so disaffected that they no longer wanted to have a voice because they felt with considerable justification that no one was listening? Stanley didn't have a majority of the people behind him. He had just done better than the other candidates, using costly marketing techniques. Stripped of campaign funds and image-makers, would he even have achieved that? What kind of democracy did they have in the US, and why did they think they were well placed to foist their particular brand of governance on other countries?

She had often heard it said that democracy was flawed, but was still the only game in town. But what if it was fatally flawed...? No one dared to ask that question, and that in itself spoke volumes. After Saddam Hussein was hanged, Iraq was supposed to adopt American-style democracy; how ironic was that? Still, she wasn't going to make waves. The system was the system. And business was business.

Just before Stanley got up to leave the table he asked, "Have you by any chance been talking to that journalist ... Lillian something ...?"

"I run into her every now and again," Evelyn answered carefully.

"She's a play-acting radical … an SJW type without any credibility."

Evelyn bridled. "Are you trying to choose my friends?"

"No." He laughed evenly. "But you're impressionable, Evelyn, and she can be quite persuasive. However, we all have to live in the real world." He left the room on that note.

Evelyn swore under her breath; the butler was still hovering. Would Lawrence be any more biddable, she wondered. She had no illusions about him. He was like one of his own missiles, armed and launched, unable to turn back or make course corrections. If he cut corners it was only because of his haste. Despite what was said about him he did have some values – whenever he gave himself half a chance to reflect. While Stanley expected it all to fall into his lap, Lawrence went out and hustled. He made things happen. Yes, she felt she knew him through and through and that was a good starting point. Maybe she could make him see sense without putting herself at risk or conceding too much to his vanity. Why had Lillian laid this burden on her?

"You didn't take much of a break, William,"

Stanley said to his deputy chairman. They sat alone at the centre of the oval table in the CASA meeting room.

"A couple of days R and R is all I need," William explained. He was glad to be back; this was his place. He would take another day or two later. Even though the rest of the committee were on vacation this was still the hub as far as he was concerned.

William outlined the budgetary options which he'd already discussed with the Treasury. The ensuing conversation very quickly focused on the bottom line.

"We can't scale back defence spending," Stanley insisted. "I think the President can be persuaded of that. He seems to have accepted the military objective of full-spectrum dominance."

"Well, we still have a problem on our hands," William said. "We can't borrow or raise taxes – too much public resistance. And slashing foreign aid won't contribute enough. So it looks like trimming social welfare."

"We have to square the circle somehow." Stanley agreed. With a silver tongs he dropped two lumps of sugar into his coffee. "What do you suggest?"

"America's role in the world has to be developed further. We have to provide leadership. Talk and carry a very big stick. That's reality. No stick, no credibility. The White House will buy that."

"And it's well known that military spending is good for the economy, especially on research. There are all sorts of technological spin-offs."

Both men nodded. The argument had legs.

"Is there any scope at all for raising taxes?" William asked, scrupulously going over the ground again. "Even ten cents on a gallon of gas would make a major contribution to reducing the Budget deficit."

Stanley shook his head. "Political suicide," he said. "We must have the most selfish consumers in the world but it's a fact of life. The welfare lobby isn't nearly as strong. But," he remembered Lawrence's point about an ageing population, "we have to go fairly easy on health spending, at least for the time being. That's how the OMB sees it too."

"I agree," William said. "Even though that could cost a fortune in the future. Every day they're developing longevity drugs. We're becoming a geriatric society. Where are we going to find the resources to keep ourselves in the luxury to which we've become accustomed?"

Stanley didn't answer. Americans had been living beyond their means for years and successive administrations had pandered to these appetites which were now out of control. Reluctantly he had to agree with the ultimate solution which Lawrence had proposed. It was only fair that client states should pay Uncle Sam for protecting them. And as the protection improved on foot of new weapons systems, the payments would have to be increased. But this was not something he was prepared to discuss even with William, not yet at least.

The conversation turned to the next election and William raised the question of whether it was wise to rely to such an extent on Kaltronics for funding. Surely there was a need to diversify?

"I've got that covered," Stanley said.

"How?" It was rare for William to ask such a direct question and, as he expected, Stanley didn't respond. He believed that although William was loyal enough, there were circumstances in which he could be compromised, maybe even to the point of breaking ranks. Stanley knew that only too well, and he also had that contingency covered.

CHAPTER 11

HAVING GONE TO a concert one night in the Lincoln Center – Riccardo Muti conducting – and to an Irish pub (with the O'Malleys) on another night, Maura felt she could agree to visit one museum at least. Patrick chose the Jewish museum, which was dominated by memorabilia of the holocaust. It was unlike any museum Maura had ever visited. Although it was quite crowded there was a hushed atmosphere; indeed, some elderly women were weeping silently. Most of the rooms were dark except for the exhibition cases which were lit from within. One room was in complete darkness and the visitors were given torches before entering it. The beams from the torches splayed randomly as the visitors shuffled uncertainly, searching out the exhibits. The effect was one of helplessness followed by shocked awareness.

They were silent for a while after they left the museum.

"Are you Jewish" Maura asked him as they walked along the pavement.

"No. Why do you ask?"

"I thought it … affected you. Especially the gold rings…" She was referring to an electronic sculpture which produced on screen the sights and sounds of gold rings being thrown one by one into a pile. A gust of dusty wind whipped round the corner of a building almost knocking her over. It whined like the ricochet of a bullet. She almost linked his arm to steady herself.

"Yes," he admitted. "The mass graves and gas ovens are beyond our comprehension. You can only get at the horror indirectly … Those rings somehow brought it home … I can't explain it exactly." His breath condensed in the frosty air. "The holocaust will always mark the last century. No country is free of blame. France did little to protect its Jewish population. Britain refused to accept Jewish immigrants. We can only hope that this century will be better."

She studied the dark narrow face, the almost cowled eyes and suddenly she was a little wiser.

"You … this operation of yours … is actually supposed … to do good?" Her voice went up on a note of incredulity. This possibility had not occurred to her before.

"Of course." He seemed almost offended by her tone.

"Good god." She uttered a malicious barking laugh. "I don't believe it. You actually think that?"

"Yes." He was taken aback by the extent of her surprise.

"Can I point out something to you? You don't kidnap and kill people to do good. I apologise for stating the obvious but maybe you don't get it."

Her sarcasm was wasted on him. "Sometimes the end justifies the means," he said evenly.

"Never." She shook her head. "Never."

"What if Hitler had been assassinated at the beginning of the war?"

"That was different. There are no Hitlers around nowadays."

"No?"

"No," she replied with some irritation. Out of the corner of her eye she could see a group of vagrants huddled around a makeshift brazier. One of them did a little lurching dance, probably to keep warm or to keep his heart up.

"Maybe we don't find out until it is too late. A monster may appear to be human for a long time. The difficulty is finding out when the monstrosity begins. Before too much suffering is caused."

"And you have the gift of foresight?"

He moved aside to let an elderly couple pass by. "It's not too difficult to make predictions when you know the people in power. And I don't mean Trump. He talks tough but he lacks real power, just like Obama before him. "

"And you know the real power-brokers?" she asked suddenly, trying to badger some information out of him. "Who in particular?" She followed up quickly, trying to keep the momentum going.

"I can't tell you that."

"Why not? Who am I going to tell?"

"It's better that you don't know. For your sake." He gave what, in other circumstances, she might have deemed to be a shy smile.

"Don't go all noble on me."

"Sorry."

She did a double take. What kind of shape-shifter was she dealing with? He just wouldn't stay in character. They could have been two people walking home from an unsuccessful date, sullen and resentful but wanting to make amends. She was intrigued by him but infuriated by the way he defied categorisation; it made a difficult situation worse, infinitely worse.

"Jesus, don't apologise," she said brusquely. "You're a kidnapper and a murderer." She needed to remind herself as much as him.

"I suppose so." He sank his hands further into his pockets and walked on with his head bowed against the wind.

A boy on a man's errand, she thought, or a well-meaning fanatic. Either could be as dangerous as hell. "That's right. There's no supposing about it."

"But I mean you no harm." They turned into the hotel and went up in the elevator. "I…I wish you well…"

This was the last straw. "Do you know what my … Harold and I have been through for the last week or so? Have you any idea what you've put us through?"

"I … can imagine." He couldn't very well apologise again but he was genuinely sorry that Maura, of all people, had to bear the brunt of his mission. She was a sincere and kind woman; he had seen tears come to her eyes in the museum. For some reason he had always associated blue eyes with frankness and honesty – maybe because brown was associated with the earth whereas blue belonged with the sky.

"No, you can't." She stabbed two fingers against his shoulder. "You haven't enough imagination. What you did was cruel."

"I know, Maura… If there had been any other way…" He gave a helpless shrug.

"There's always another way." She noticed that he had used her name; it came as something of a shock.

"Sometimes you must break eggs…"

"God. Omelettes now … Don't give me that." She followed him into the suite. "Who are you to judge? You're not…" Suddenly his face loomed in front of hers and she was in his arms. He was kissing her and she was responding with little hesitation, drawing his tongue into her mouth. Her heart was pounding. She didn't know who started it. The question was where would it end.

Half asleep, she tossed and turned, agonising over another question which was vague, unformed. Suddenly it came into sharp focus as she woke fully. Oh, Christ, she had ... they had ... She got out of bed and had to stand still for several seconds to recover from a dizzy spell. She went into the small kitchen and steadied herself against the worktop, staring into the stainless steel sink. Tears came into her eyes. She tried to wipe them away with one hand while holding on to the worktop with the other. Then she heard his voice behind her.

"Don't Maura. It's all right." It had crossed his mind that she might have consented as a means of manipulating him, but now he realized how foolish that thought had been. It just wasn't in her nature.

"It's not all right. It's wrong ... wrong ... all wrong..." She started to weep.

He was badly shaken by her reaction; had he forced himself on her? He summoned up the courage to ask her straight out.

She ran the cold tap and splashed water in her face as if it were a cleansing ritual. "No," she said abruptly. "I take responsibility for my own actions, however badly judged."

He put a hand on her shoulder and gently tried to turn her towards him. She shrugged him off.

"Then I don't...understand...You can't deny..."

"Don't … don't start that. I hate myself for what happened. I made love with the man who kidnapped my husband. It's reprehensible."

He stood beside her for a long time in silence and then said in a low voice, "It happened. And I'm glad."

"And it's over."

"I don't think so … I hope not."

"You've put … your brand on me … Is that it?" She refused to look at him.

"No. How can you say that?"

She tore off a sheet of kitchen paper and wiped her eyes with it. "It's over."

"I told you last night that…"

She held up both hands. "I don't want to remember … I'm not having an affair with a … I'm not having an affair."

"I'm sorry if I've upset you or…" he searched for a word, "…compromised you…"

"Oh god!" She didn't know whether to laugh or cry. "You didn't 'compromise' me, as you put it. I did it all by myself. A moment of madness … I can take responsibility, you know." She filled the kettle with water and switched it on. It seemed an incongruously homely thing to do.

"Then, you're not mad … at me?"

"You, me, everything. How the hell do you think I feel? My husband … in a cellar somewhere…" She became incoherent. "…the ultimate betrayal … Don't you see…?"

"No," he said. "No, I don't see…"

"Wh-a-a-at…" She finally turned to face him. The morning light from the window hit her painfully between the eyes.

"He doesn't deserve you." He caught her wrist as she swung at him. "I've watched … studied him. He didn't ask about you … He's selfish and … how do you say … a prig. You owe him nothing…"

"How dare you!" Her head was splitting. "It's none of your business." She wrestled her hand free of his grip.

"You haven't denied it," Patrick said.

"Of course I deny it. Now please leave me alone."

"He will not be harmed … I give you my word…"

"You can't say that … you don't know what will happen…" She rushed into the bedroom and wept silently. She felt as if she had lost her footing and fallen into a world of confusion and uncertainty.

The indefatigable Clare O'Malley saved the day again by whisking them off on another jaunt, which was probably the perfect distraction – a helicopter tour of Manhattan with the odd foray into Queens and Brooklyn.

"I'm not so sure about this," Tim O'Malley said as he was about to board the chopper.

"In you get," Clare said, giving him a vigorous push. "This'll cure your fear of heights."

"How're you folks today?" The pilot greeted them jauntily, while a ground steward buckled them into their seats. He gave a brief outline of the itinerary they would follow and then turned to the controls while continuing to chat to them over his shoulder.

They sat facing each other in the narrow confines of the helicopter. Tim didn't look at all happy and checked the clasp of his seatbelt several times as well as the bolts that secured the all-too-transparent doors.

"OK, folks," the pilot said. "We're ready to depart the fix." The main rotor blade began its rhythmic purr overhead.

"These things have been known to fall out of the sky. No wings … can't even glide." Tim kneaded his hands, which felt numb.

The two women laughed but Patrick tried to reassure him, "Even if they lose power they can auto-rotate down. You know, like a sycamore seed…" The pilot confirmed this with what passed for a reassuring smile.

"Yeah, well I'd prefer to be in something more substantial than a sycamore seed." Tim was unimpressed.

They ascended slowly into the air, then went forward at an angle, the horizon dipping violently on one side. From The Bronx they headed east over Long Island Sound then south over Oyster Bay, Long Beach and Jamaica Bay. The chopper swooped and soared and although Tim had some bad moments, the majestic perspective and enthusiastic commentary of the pilot seemed to take the edge off his fear. They passed over Governor's Island and proceeded north along the Hudson, where they could see the transatlantic liners, as well as an aircraft carrier, tied up at the piers. Then they criss-crossed Manhattan itself, virtually flying between the sky-scrapers, sometimes seeing families, office workers and steeplejacks going about their daily business. They were like exotic birds living in the canopy of a rain forest. It was a different world which went beyond anything that virtual reality could offer and it brought an adrenalin rush that was intoxicating. There was little conversation; even Clare was too absorbed to talk. Maura felt light-headed, the memory of her recent experience expunged for the moment.

The pilot then brought them to see the skyscraper that replaced the twin towers. He told them it was called the One World Trade Center and, at 1,250 feet tall, was the highest building in the Western Hemisphere. Then he lapsed into a respectful silence. His passengers were impressed, and Tim, asked if it was also called Freedom Tower.

"Yes, sir," the pilot replied.

Patrick held his peace. In his view, 9/11 was a false flag operation carried out by the CIA and FEMA to frighten the public and 'justify' wars in the oil-rich Middle-East. He had read most of the books by scientists and engineers. Ordinary commercial planes could not have penetrated into steel buildings, and they could not have collapsed into their own footprints. The crash scenes at the Pentagon and at Shanksville were a joke. Missiles and explosives had undoubtedly been used. He still could not understand how gullible Americans were, or how patriotic. Maybe they just could not bring themselves to believe such an ugly truth. Did they not know that the CIA had undertaken over three hundred black ops since its creation, or did they simply not care?

After they landed they went for coffee and, with the exception of Patrick, remained in a state of euphoria as if they hadn't fully come down to earth.

"What a blast!" Clare repeated for the third time, her face still flushed with excitement. "Not too bad, Tim?"

"Well, I survived," he conceded.

"You're my hero. You'll be able to climb a ladder now. No excuse for not cleaning the gutters anymore."

"I wouldn't go that far. Let's not get carried away."

"Did you enjoy it?" Patrick asked Maura.

"Yes … It was an experience," she replied for form's sake. The diversion had had the desired effect but now it was well and truly over.

"And you, Harold?" Clare was determined to carry out a complete inventory.

"Great," Patrick said and then added as if more was expected, "I've flown in them before."

"Oh, where?"

"Africa." He knew he would have to elaborate a little. "In some areas the roads are so bad you have to take a chopper or a light aircraft."

"Do you know Africa well?" Tim inquired.

Patrick hesitated. "Not very well … My brother worked there for some years … I used to visit him." He wanted to change the subject but nothing came to him. He had to behave socially, but ordinary conversation was fraught with risk.

"It must have been a wonderful experience," Clare put in. "Did you enjoy it, Maura?"

"I…"

"That was before we met," Patrick interjected quickly.

"Typical," Tim snorted. "No jaunts after marriage. I know that story."

Clare elbowed him in the ribs. "Listen to the poor martyr."

"Well, I don't know about you," Tim announced, "But I could murder a burger or two." He hadn't been able to eat before the trip and now felt ravenous. The others declined, but agreed to have coffee while he ate.

Clare looked at Maura more than once, wondering why she had become so quiet. Was it possible that she was afraid of heights as well, or was there something else going on?

CHAPTER 12

LAWRENCE REGARDED BOARD meetings as a waste of time. If his fellow directors agreed with him they were redundant; if they disagreed they were obnoxious and had to be persuaded or ignored. The latter ran the risk of alienating them, especially as diplomacy was not his strong suit.

This particular meeting wasn't too trying, however. They dealt quickly with a proposal to acquire an engineering company in Ohio and they had no difficulty about accepting the East European order after Lawrence reassured them about the ability to pay in dollars.

The most important item on the agenda was the research investment plan and it also proved to be the most contentious. Three directors adopted a cautious approach, fearing the risks involved in creating a weapons system that was based on such new technology. One of them pointed out that the Manhattan Project worked only because there was no budget constraint whatsoever. He feared that Kaltronics could be left with a large burden of debt and egg on its face. The issue was batted to and fro for a long time. Technical and financial experts came and went, displaying figures, graphs and projections on a screen at one end of the room. Bob Carraway, having been thoroughly rehearsed by

Lawrence in advance of the meeting, made an excellent presentation, but the three recalcitrant directors continued to voice reservations.

Seated at the head of the polished oval table, Lawrence grew more and more impatient. He had no intention of trying to explain the geo-political background to them. Most of it was classified and in any case many of the directors sat on boards of companies which could be said to be rivals of Kaltronics, at least indirectly. He stood up and paced while the financial controller was going over cash-flow projections.

Out of the corner of his eye he could see the portrait of the founder, his great-grandfather, dominating the boardroom. The painter had caught the stern look but not the soft heart which lay behind it. He had, Lawrence reflected, been tough enough where business was concerned and although he set high standards for the family, he never imposed sanctions for failure to meet them. The business had of course flourished during the war but when the Nazis came to power he had refused to cooperate in so far as that was possible. He belonged to that line of rough, brilliant but strangely naive arms experts which included Nobel, Oppenheimer and Feynman, and towards the end of his life he had been plagued by feelings of guilt. Lawrence knew from family folklore, that his father had tried to reason with the old man but by that time he was sinking into senile dementia and could not be released from intimations of damnation which undoubtedly hastened his death.

Feeling that the board had had ample time to debate the investment issue, Lawrence decided to bring it to a head. He summarised the arguments for and against and finally drew, rather unfairly, on his own past record.

"Have I," he asked, "Ever misdirected the board on a strategic issue of this magnitude?"

There was a murmur of protest indicating that he had no need to ask such a question. They trusted his judgement implicitly.

"This is an extraordinary opportunity," he went on. "If we don't grasp it now, others will. We have a slight … head start and I believe we should exploit it fully. In this business you can't stand still. If you do, that in itself is a huge risk. It is important to be one step ahead of the competition at every stage." He continued until he felt the dissent begin to melt away.

After some token caveats, the cautious directors didn't pursue the matter further, though they seemed a bit miffed by his tactics.

The next item was a personnel matter, involving industrial relations. Lawrence gave a brief outline of the situation and modestly asked for the board's agreement to allow him to enter into negotiations. He would of course revert to them with a progress report. Agreed. The directors had little stomach for the hurly burly of industrial relations.

Some odds and ends were raised under Any Other Business and were quickly disposed of. The directors packed their attaché cases, exchanged pleasantries and gradually drifted away.

Lawrence asked Bob Carraway to contact the Personnel Chief and meet him in his office in an hour.

When he got back to his office his secretary gave him a list of people who had called him, including a Mrs. Evelyn Ralston.

"I believe," the secretary said in hushed tones, "That she is the wife of congressman Ralston.

"I'll call her back," Lawrence said with a grin. "What else, Rose?"

"A lot of texts and e-mail messages. I've sorted and downloaded most of them onto your computer."

"Good. I'll look at them tonight."

She nodded, her tawny hair falling forward over her face. "Your wife also called to say she was going to St. Lucia for another week or so."

"Lucky for some," Lawrence said.

"Yes, sir." Rose returned his smile. "I've been checking your e-diary, and there seems to be a clash on January thirty-first. When you pencilled in Mr. Cantrell of Conductive Alloys you may have … forgotten about the event in Washington…"

"And I have to go to that?"

"Well, as you know, it is being hosted by

KNYBS and you did promise … They're expecting you to say a few words…"

"Oh god. And the press will be there I suppose?"

"Yes, sir. The PR Department is very enthusiastic. Gerry says the response to date is fantastic, that you can't put a price on that kind of goodwill…"

"The company that cares," Lawrence said as an aside. Although he had little time for spin-doctors except in relation to elections, he was intrigued by their mind-set. They seemed to believe that with the proper campaign they could make a silk purse out of a sow's ear. It was a ludicrous form of paranoia. He looked across the desk at Rose, who was patiently waiting for his decision.

"Put Mr. Cantrell back to the New Year . I must go to the ball," he quipped. He noted that she seemed relieved. The PR Department must have been putting pressure on her. "But tell Gerry to keep the press to a minimum." Several years ago he had reluctantly agreed to give a brief interview to a respected journalist who somehow managed to blow it up into a five-page spread full of speculation masquerading as truth, including a thinly veiled suggestion that his forebears had been Nazi sympathisers. Of course there had been other reports over the years but he gave no interviews as such. He knew how the liberal folk of the fourth estate would love to do a hatchet job on his core business. Fortunately he had some protection on that front: national security. That had helped him run Michael Moore and his ilk off the premises several times.

Occasionally the hacks and paparazzi tried to invade his privacy and sometimes he had to give them the odd morsel, like the fact that he worked a fifteen-hour day or that all his suits were made from the same cloth. It was like throwing pieces of meat off the sled to slow down pursuing bears. Every time he read about himself in print or saw a piece on TV he cringed. But at least it served as a sort of smoke screen. They hadn't really come that close to his role in the political process. He wasn't ashamed of that; in his book democracy wouldn't function without big business behind it. It cost almost $2 billion dollars to get a President elected. Politicians didn't object; why should he?

Left to themselves, politicians couldn't run a whelk stall. The entire system was flawed and, without the help of capitalists, it would grind to a halt. Utopia was not an option, whatever the liberals of the press might believe, and the radicals like Noam Chomsky and Chris Hedges couldn't find their way to the bathroom. America had to remain strong. It was a historical imperative. European countries had had their chance and blown it. Religions, which used to provide moral leadership, had imploded under the weight of pedophilia, fundamentalism and terrorism. America had to carry the standard for successive generations. To do that properly the military had to be provided with the best hi-tech weapons available.

There was of course another reason for hiding his light under a bushel: personal security. That didn't weigh too heavily on him but Bob Carraway insisted on two of the firm's security staff living at his house in San Francisco.

"Well, if there's nothing else…" Rose was saying.

"What …? Oh, that's fine, Rose. Thanks."

After she left, he recalled how she used to shop for Christmas and anniversary presents for his wife. She would circle various items from the up-market catalogues and present them to him with little comments pencilled in the margins. It was uncanny how she got it right every time. Amanda had given him credit for taste and thoughtfulness … until she found out about the method he had been using. It had caused one of their many rows. Amanda simply failed to understand that he couldn't have handled it any other way. He had tried to explain to her the necessity for time-management but that was a foreign concept to her, and she persisted in believing it symbolised where she ranked in his priorities. After that, everything he did or said seemed to acquire symbolic value. Potentially dangerous signifiers lurked everywhere. Casual comments could explode in his face. It was as if they spoke different languages or rather different dialects of the same language. He was surprised by her reaction because it was supposed to be a marriage of convenience. Perhaps she wanted more from it than that. But he couldn't deliver more because of business commitments and the responsibility he felt for almost a hundred and fifty thousand employees.

And of course he couldn't get Evelyn out of his system; they were two sides of the same coin. He probably shouldn't have married Amanda at all. There was a lot to be said for celibacy; the Catholic Church wasn't completely wrong about that. Still, Amanda seemed to be happy enough now, running with the jet set; if she needed him at all it was as a sort of back-stop. They both knew where they stood and they had mellowed into a reasonable, passionless compromise – civil when they met, slightly relieved when they parted. It could have been a lot worse.

Even the sound of Evelyn's voice could quicken his pulse – as it did when he returned her call.

"Why didn't you … stay longer when you were in Washington last week?" she asked.

"Well, it was a flying visit," he said. He was going to say something about Stanley's hovering presence but thought better of it. He wondered why she had called him.

"Are you still keeping downwind of the

media?" she asked with a faint taunt in her voice.

"Doing my best," he laughed. "But it's hard enough to throw them off the scent. You're not too successful in that area. The papers out here are full of your activities."

"It goes with the job," she said ruefully. "Speaking of which, the end-of-year ball is attracting huge publicity. I presume you're going to put in an appearance…"

"Yes. As a matter of fact I was discussing it a few minutes ago…"

"And Amanda of course…"

"Oh I doubt that. She'll probably be on some yacht in warmer climes working on her tan."

"Well, we must raise a glass together," Evelyn said.

"Absolutely. Go over old times."

"It should be good fun."

"I hope so."

"I hope so too, Lawrence."

For a while after the conversation ended, a vague smile lay over his features. So they were going to meet again … His reverie was broken by the appearance of Bob Carraway and the chief of personnel, John Franklin. The three men sat down at the conference table.

"The Board meeting went well," Bob said.

"I guess it will hold them for another month," Lawrence replied. "Now what's this personnel matter? Who wants what and why?"

He felt unusually light-hearted after his conversation with Evelyn.

John Franklin took his cue. "The engineers, metallurgists and systems people are claiming that the pay differential between them and their academic counterparts has been eroded by fifteen percent. They are seeking full restoration."

"I see." Lawrence reflected on how childish these scientists could be. Relativities were all that counted. If their colleagues in universities got a pay increase they wanted the same. A form of peer pressure, he supposed. "So what would that mean on their actual pay rates?" he asked.

John consulted the screen of his laptop. "About seven percent across the board.

"And in absolute terms?"

Bob Carraway took this question. "I ran it by Accounts. It comes out at about three and a half million dollars a year."

Lawrence shook his head. "Offer them two percent."

John seemed uneasy. "They're in a fairly good bargaining position," he said. "They know about the investment plan and they are pretty mobile as you know. We've lost a number to Wall Street as quants already. Others are being head-hunted as we speak. Some of these banks and securities houses are offering considerable hello-money..."

"I can't believe the banks are back into

financial engineering after the last mess they made." Lawrence recalled one of the top investors in the country referring to derivative products as weapons of mass destruction. Part of the problem was that mathematical types had no street smarts.

Bob rubbed his receding hairline. "Banks and their regulators never learn. There's another risk of course. We could lose our guys to Silicon Valley as well, even though our pay rates are reasonably competitive with those."

"OK, John. I think you should start at two percent and make them sweat blood up to an absolute max of four percent. They know that we can recruit new graduates for a helluva lot less."

"Morale is … poor…" John fought a rearguard action, although he suspected it wouldn't cut any ice.

"How do you measure that?" Lawrence asked.

"Feedback … keeping in touch…"

"But how do you measure it?"

"Well, it can't be measured as such … there's no metric…"

"Then forget about it," Lawrence said. He had no time for such nebulous concepts. "So we're clear on the offer?"

Both men nodded and made to leave.

"One other thing," Lawrence said. "One of our rocket scientists, Yamey, published an article in an academic journal. He came very close to revealing the electronic configuration of our new guidance system. Speak to him about it."

"Of course," John Franklin said. "But it's a very obscure journal. Only a few academics could even read it…"

"A few too many," Lawrence said. "If Yamey wants to make a name for himself he can work for a university. But right now he's under contract to Kaltronics. Remind him of that and of intellectual property rights. We're not in the business of increasing the sum of human knowledge. Talk to him."

"Yes, sir."

When the two men had reached the safety of the corridor they exchanged glances.

"He's not exactly a pushover," John said.

"But look how he's grown the company," Bob said. "OK, you mightn't enjoy going for a drink with him. I guess he can't afford to be popular. And for god's sake, put the frighteners on Yamey. Anyone else would have sacked the geeky little bastard on the spot."

When they reached the end of the corridor they split up and went their separate ways.

Though buoyed up by the phone call from Evelyn, Lawrence still had a lot of work to get through. Later that day he would have to meet a general from Quantico whom he had flown out – the military brass liked their little travel perks – and bring him to the firing range to lay on a display of the latest hand-held artillery. If a sale was in the offing he would then have to get the lawyers to draw up contract documents. He probably wouldn't get home before ten. His housekeeper would have a light meal waiting for him. Then he would hit the sheets, setting the alarm for 5.30 a.m. Fortunately, the PR guys would take the general out on the town if that was his wish; they tended to come alive at night like vampire pimps. But at least they saved Lawrence that particular chore.

It had taken him years to learn how to delegate and that was only because the company reached a certain size and there simply was no alternative. He was still an engineer and a manufacturer at heart and he liked nothing better than to visit the factory floor and watch the components come together into the finished product. He believed that the production of physical goods was the only economic reality. He had little time for paper pushers, lawyers, middle managers – many of whom he had stripped out of the organisation – and financiers. He regarded bankers as touts in good suits who used the jargon of the marketplace only to hide the superficiality of their trade. They were vandals at heart, fee-mongers and asset-strippers who knew they would be bailed out when they messed up – as they did in 2008. The most hard-bitten criminals could give them lessons in morality.

In fact Lawrence had a sneaking regard for honest crooks. Once when he was in Rome with

Amanda he had gone on his own to see the Forum – she had gone shopping. He was mugged by two ruffians in broad daylight. They held him at knife point and took his wallet and watch. Then, gratuitously, they roughed him up, dislocating his left shoulder. When they moved away from him he took out the small hand-gun, bought for an exorbitant price from the Cosa Nostra, and, from a kneeling position, he took aim. He could easily have wounded one of them if not both. But he didn't fire. Not because he was afraid of the consequences – he was too well connected for that. He wasn't exactly sure why he hesitated but it had something to do with the fact that they were honest hustlers. They took a risk and would probably spend half their lives in jail anyway.

By contrast, bankers and financiers took no risks but indulged in legalised theft every minute of every day. They were the bottom feeders of the food chain. He could never understand how the Gnomes of Zurich had such a squeaky-clean image when they lived off the sweat and blood of millions of oppressed peoples the world over. All the top American banks had plush offices in Miami for laundering drug money, and for no other reason.

America still had its work ethic, its belief in giving value for a dollar. It had its share of snake-oil salesmen, white-collar criminals and of course politicians but, in general, the system operated on the basis of honest toil and genuine risk-taking. What worried him more than anything was the possibility that these values might disappear as the sense of practical patriotism went into decline. There was evidence that this was happening. One incident in particular stuck in his mind. On a previous visit to Washington he had gone for a walk along the Mall and stopped in front of the Lincoln Memorial. It was virtually an act of homage and as he stood there contemplating the awe-inspiring statue of Lincoln, his attention was drawn to the sight of a young man relieving himself on a corner of the steps.

"Stop it!" Lawrence snapped.

"Say what …?"

"You're desecrating a national monument."

"What's it to you …?" He continued to urinate.

"We're both citizens. I said stop it. Now!" Lawrence was aghast. How could anyone do that?

"Fuck you, man." He zipped up his flies and charged up the steps with bunched fists. When he got to the top step he decided to use his feet instead and aimed a vicious kick in the direction of Lawrence's groin. Jumping back in the nick of time, Lawrence caught the descending foot in his hands and held his man off balance. His would-be assailant hopped on his other leg and swung his fists wildly, trying to land a punch.

"Cut it out!" Lawrence yelled.

"You motherfucker … you dead meat…" The youth produced a knife from his back pocket; one of the slashes caught Lawrence on the left arm but didn't draw blood. He was about to follow it up when Lawrence twisted the foot and suddenly pushed it away from him. The man lost his balance as well as the knife and went tumbling down the steps where he lay winded.

On that occasion he had also gone to see the Vietnam War Memorial. He was appalled by it and saddened at the same time. It was black and half buried, like a large tombstone, symbolising all of the half-baked, ambivalent attitudes of the authorities towards that particular conflict, which must have been one of the bleakest episodes in American history. It was a war they could never win (short of nuclear strikes) because, in Lawrence's view, the appropriate munitions had not yet been invented. Almost half a century later that was no longer the case and Lawrence was proud of having had something to do with that. There was, however, more to be done, much more …

As he prepared for his meeting with the general from Quantico Marine Corps Base, he allowed himself to be distracted by thoughts of meeting Evelyn in DC at the end of the year. He couldn't remember the last time he had looked forward to something in quite that way.

CHAPTER 13

"I JUST DON'T know," Clare O'Malley mused aloud as she teased her hair in front of the dressing table.

"I don't either." Tim lay on the bed sipping a cold beer.

"What don't you know?"

"Whatever it is you're on about."

"Well, it is kind of odd." Clare rummaged in her cosmetics bag for an eye-liner. With a little cry of triumph she picked it out and leant forward to be closer to the mirror.

Tim punched the pillows in exasperation and sat up. "What in god's name are you mumbling about?"

"Those two."

"Which two?"

"Maura and Harold. Who else?"

"Oh god, what about them?"

"I'm not sure," Clare said thoughtfully. It's just a feeling…"

"You're doing it to me again." Tim ran a hand through his hair. "You're trying to drive me mad. Isn't that it? Then have me committed and take all the money."

"What money? Oh, don't be so melodramatic. You must have noticed something too…"

"Something? What something? Spit it out,

woman."

"There's something odd about them. I can't put my finger on it exactly…" She paused to seek inspiration from the ceiling. "It's as if … they're not really close or something…"

"Ah, that's just British formality. Stiff upper lip and all that. They're probably at it hammer and tongs in the boudoir even as we speak."

"No-o-o, I don't think it's that. It's got nothing to do with sex … They don't seem relaxed … in each other's company." She turned to face him and her eyes widened with sudden insight. "Harold doesn't give out to her…"

"What? Christ, I've heard everything now."

"You know what I mean. He doesn't pull her leg or kid around with her … or take her to task … It's not normal."

"You're as mad as a March hare. And," he looked at his watch, "you've made us late as usual."

"That's the sort of thing, I mean," Clare said triumphantly.

"What is?"

"What you've just said … Sniping and sparring and all that." She shadow-boxed in his direction to indicate the kind of sparring she had in mind.

"I give up." He passed a hand over his head to indicate that this was beyond his simple understanding, then he got off the bed and started to look for his shoes.

After throwing off the blanket, Patrick got up from the sofa, paused for a while at one of the windows in the sitting room of the suite and looked out at the city which, like himself, couldn't sleep. He passed by Maura's bedroom as quietly as he could, and went into the kitchen where he put on the kettle and sat down, trying to sort out those disconcerting thoughts that had kept him awake. He would somehow have to put Maura out of his head and re-focus himself. It was almost Christmas and shortly after that he would be in Washington where he simply could not afford any distractions.

Whatever her reasons, it was probably just as well that Maura had spurned him after that night. If only he could stop agonising about what those reasons might have been … and if he could forget, even temporarily, those blue eyes in close-up and the softness of her skin … It was all crazy of course and doomed to failure. But why then had she slept with him, knowing that she would regret it? It was way over his head; maybe in time he would come to understand … He whirled around as he heard the door open.

"I'm … sorry…" Maura was equally surprised and stood frozen for a moment, drawing her robe about her. She made to leave.

"No, I'll go…" He got to his feet. "If you want to use…"

"Stay. It's all right. I just couldn't…"

"I was going to make some tea … Would you like a cup?" he asked. As if on cue, the kettle came to the boil.

"OK." She sat down and rearranged the robe around her knees.

He stood with his back to her, pouring the boiling water into the cups in which he had put tea bags. He put the sugar bowl and a jug of milk on the table, then placed a small spoon in each saucer.

"Would you like a biscuit?" he inquired.

"No thank you."

He placed her cup on the table in front of her and sat down with his own. There was little eye contact. Whenever he glanced at her she was looking away. She took a sip of tea and shuddered; it was much too tannic.

"You don't like it?" he asked.

"It's a little … strong."

He went towards her to retrieve the cup. "I'll make more…"

"There's no need…" His face was close to hers but she didn't move away. He kissed her gently on the cheek.

"I'm sorry," he said.

"So am I."

They sipped their tea in silence.

The hotel put on a great Christmas programme. Maura discovered that she and Patrick had a shared sense of what Christmas meant. At first she felt unworthy to enter into the spirit of it because of what had happened; she was an adulteress after all, though Patrick vehemently denied that.

The hotel management probably overdid it a little on Christmas Day itself. Presents were distributed immediately after breakfast by Art, their friendly courier and minder. Mercifully, he wasn't got up as Santa Claus. The eggnog began to flow shortly afterwards. Maura, dressed in a russet sweater and ski pants, linked Patrick; they even kissed under the mistletoe. Accompanied by the O'Malleys and a few other couples, they went to mass in St. Patrick's Cathedral, which rang to the rafters with the sound of carol-singing. They returned in time for lunch, which consisted of all the traditional fare: turkey and ham with chestnut stuffing, sweet potatoes, brandy-soaked plum pudding. They wore funny hats and pulled crackers. One Australian couple, who said they were 'partied out', fell asleep in their chairs. But most of the guests felt a buzz of excitement; there was an added air of expectancy about the imminent trip to Washington.

Clare O'Malley noticed a change in

Maura's demeanour towards Patrick. "I'm glad you made it up," she whispered at one point, giving a knowing look.

"Was it that obvious?" Maura asked, though she was far from certain that anything had been resolved.

"We all have occasional little tiffs," Clare said. "Goes with the territory. And keeps us on our toes." She gave a conspiratorial wink.

Maura was conscious of looking at Patrick through new eyes. She saw what a good listener he was, how he entered into things in his own quiet way without drawing attention to himself. She had watched him shaving that morning; it seemed to be a major operation scraping off that strong black stubble that reached down to his Adam's apple. Now, already, he had a blue-tinged six o'clock shadow which accentuated his jaw line. She couldn't quite describe the colour of his eyes: brownish certainly but she wanted to be more specific. For some reason she wanted to label the exact shade. Oak, possibly.

After lunch they went for a walk on their own in Central Park. They were well wrapped up against the cold. When he tried to take hold of her hand she bridled but softened the rebuke by a sympathetic glance.

"Christmas is really a time for kids," she said. "I think adults can only fully appreciate it through their eyes."

Patrick agreed. He used to visit his sister-in-law in Macon; she had two children and without them the occasion would have meant little. After some hesitation he told her how his brother Jean had died in Africa. She was the only person he had ever told. She listened in silence. For the first time she understood what it was that drove him.

"Maybe ... you should try to ... put it behind you," she said gently, knowing how inadequate her words were.

He shook his head slowly; he couldn't aspire to Maura's Buddhist-like serenity, though he admired her for it. She didn't pursue the matter. They walked by the open-air theatre, which seemed strangely forlorn; on their other side was a lake which was partly iced over. Dusk began to draw in and infused the air with a biting chill. They decided to retrace their steps.

When they got back to the hotel the party was in full swing. They had hot punch in front of the fire, listening with some amusement to a German's guttural and quick tempo rendition of 'Silent Night'. There was a break in the proceedings during which Art set about arranging people in groups.

"I hope we're not going to play party games," Maura said. "No, it's for the media," Art explained. It seemed that some press photographers had been promised an opportunity to take pictures of the lucky foreigners who would soon be rubbing shoulders with the great and the good at the bash in Washington.

"Damn!" Patrick muttered.

Maura immediately realised his predicament. "Go to the loo," she said.

"What?"

"The toilet."

He slipped away and she joined the largest group, which posed for several photographs. Afterwards names and addresses were taken and written into notebooks. Maura simply said, "Mr. and Mrs. Crowther, Hertfordshire, England." She wondered if that had been wise. But what was done was done and she put it out of her head.

"Harold missed it. Is he camera shy or what?"

Maura turned around to see Tim O'Malley at her elbow.

"Yes," she said. "A call of nature. All this rich food." She noticed that Tim was a little tipsy.

"Hasn't he got a French accent?" he inquired out of the blue.

"What?"

"I was having a chat with that Canadian couple and they reckoned that Harold has a sort of a French accent."

"Very observant," Patrick said, having just returned. "I lived for several years in Paris."

"Good for you," Tim said.

"Global village," Maura put in. "We're a

very cosmopolitan lot nowadays."

Tim beckoned Clare to join them and picked up a fresh glass of whiskey. "We'll be worn out before the grand hooley," he said.

"You will anyway," Clare said. "The way you're putting away that stuff."

"Christmas times," Tim replied. "You have to celebrate. There's no choice in the matter. It's expected." He raised his glass. "To us, the chosen ones."

"The over-indulging ones." Clare patted his paunch and then observed ruefully that she had put on several pounds since the holiday began. "I feel like a broiler fowl. Maybe we're part of some horrible experiment, being fattened up by aliens…"

"I know what you mean." Maura laughed. "It's a bit overpowering, suffocating almost. We should be taking some exercise. Of course, Patrick goes jogging…"

"Who?" Tim inquired, looking closely at her.

"Harold. Sorry, I must be getting tight."

"You do?" Clare asked.

"Not every day," Patrick answered. "There's a heated swimming pool off the lobby. It's good. You should try that."

The suggestion failed to carry the day. Tim said he couldn't swim a stroke and Clare demurred on the grounds that her swimming costume probably wouldn't fit her anymore.

"I know we're being spoiled rotten," Tim

said, "and we can't judge America on the basis of this experience. But it really is a great country. Look at all of us right here, right now, thanks to the generosity of corporate sponsors. What are they getting out of it? Some goodwill, probably. But basically it reflects the generosity of the American people." He became wistful, even a little maudlin. "We should've settled here years ago." He went on to say that they'd lived in England for a couple of years but there was no comparison. The English tried to be sophisticated but were in fact insecure. Loss of empire, he supposed.

"Tim!" Clare pointed out his gaffe.

"Present company excluded of course," Tim said gallantly.

"The US is nearly too powerful though," Maura offered. "A lot of responsibility goes with that sort of power."

"'Course none of the politicians are worth much," Tim said. "They're all bought and paid for. But it's the same in every country. What do you think, Harold?"

Patrick shrugged. "I don't know. It wouldn't say much for democracy…"

"Ah, democracy," Tim sighed. "The greatest myth since Adam was a boy. People like us have no say, none at all." He finished his drink and Clare quickly presented him with a glass of designer water. He made a moue at the first sip but accepted the offering without objection.

"At least there's free speech," Clare pointed out.

"Another myth," Tim declaimed. "The media are part of the establishment. They try to pretend they're not but deep down they are. They know which side their bread is buttered on. They go after small stuff like bonking bishops, sexual peccadillos and racist yobs. But they never go after the big stories." He looked to Patrick for confirmation but he simply made a see-sawing gesture with his hands as if he were trying to weigh up the evidence. The conversation then turned to political correctness and hate speech, and who decided what was incorrect and hateful.

As the evening wore on Maura began to feel that there was something sinister about the way they were being pampered. The precise image that formed in her mind was of a group of first-class passengers on the Titanic. Of course, they were also first into the lifeboats; the steerage passengers were let drown like rats. She realised with a start that she was being drawn into the landscape of Patrick's mind. Her concern for Harold abated a little; he would not be harmed. Indeed her thoughts of him now were of a faintly whimsical kind. She used to trim his nostril hair to save his patients a rather unseemly sight as they looked upwards from the dentist's chair. But he still managed to frighten the children with his formal manner. She remembered one nine-year old boy who jumped out of the chair and ran home crying with two molars half-drilled. Harold would be all right. He was already probably boring his captors to distraction. Was this rationalisation on her part? No, she didn't think so.

She tilted her face slightly upwards and their lips met. She clasped her hands around his neck and rose with him as he straightened up. Her robe fell open as she pressed herself against him. Not daring to separate, they groped and staggered their way into the bedroom. Though clearly experienced, there was some quality of innocence about him without which she might have resisted. As they fell on the bed she was committed; the sudden gravity of desire had taken over. It was sensation in its purest form; no minds needed, only hearts, lungs and loins. They groomed each other like mammals. Consequences were of no account; this was a high-stakes gamble of the flesh and nothing else mattered. It was she who curtailed the foreplay. She threw convention to the wind and, spurred on by Patrick, followed every instinct of desire into new realms. The word, 'wanton', came to her. She was wanton if that meant abandoning herself completely to the moment, to exploring in minute detail the novelty of the one body they formed. She cried out, climaxed, wept, laughed; for once in her life there were no limits and no recriminations.

It wasn't that her feelings of guilt had melted away. She had somehow risen above and mastered them. Never before had she experienced such power to give and take pleasure. She wanted him all the time. Her body ached then and later as she walked the hotel corridors or ventured out into the street. It was crazy, yes, absolute insanity; immoral, almost certainly; doomed to failure – she closed her mind to that.

CHAPTER 14

PAUL TOLD THE driver to wait and went into the chemist's shop. He handed in the prescription and asked how long it would take to make up.

"You're Mr. Harold Crowther of Hertingfordbury?" the pharmacist asked as he examined the prescription. "You're a little off the beaten track," he added.

"Yes," Paul said. "I just ran out of medication … and was worried…"

"Oh, there's no need to worry. This is a very small dose. Your doctor must be extremely cautious. I won't be a minute." The pharmacist went into the back to fill the prescription.

So, Crowther had been trying it on, Paul thought. When Harold had told him he needed pills for his heart, Paul had wondered about it. But when he produced the prescription from his wallet they decided not to take any risks; they didn't want his death on their hands. He had obviously hoped they would go to his regular pharmacist who might smell a rat and alert the authorities. And to think they had almost felt sorry for him. That pompous asshole. They'd got him some books and a battery-powered radio. They let him slop out every morning and served him meals on demand. Now this.

Before going into the cellar Paul put on a

balaclava. Harold looked up from his bed where he'd been reading. "Well, did you get them?" he asked.

Paul threw the pills at him. "Nice try," he grated.

"What do you mean?" Harold removed his glasses and gave him a haughty, professorial look.

"Don't play innocent," Paul snapped.

Harold thought for a while and then asked, "Did you go to Remington's pharmacy?"

"Of course not. Do you think we're idiots?"

Harold examined the logo on the paper bag and knew that he'd been foiled. "It was worth a try," he said. He was now so sure of his survival that he didn't bother to dissemble. Paul wanted to hit him. The day before yesterday he'd gone into the cellar just as Harold was rising from the bucket, pulling up his trousers. He upbraided him for not knocking. Paul felt like laughing; the man had such notions about himself even when he was shitting in a bucket. Now Paul didn't feel like laughing and was sorry they'd gone out of their way to calm his fears. They should have kept him in a state of terror.

"When the hell am I getting out of here?" Harold demanded.

"When the time is right," Paul answered tersely. "And not before."

"You said yesterday it would be a matter of days." Harold took off his glasses and pointed them accusingly at the other man.

"That was yesterday. Before you played this stupid little trick."

"So, I'm to be punished is that it?"

"Figure it out for yourself." Paul made to leave.

"My wife had better come back in one piece," Harold said darkly.

"I don't think you're in a position to make demands. If I were you I'd keep my mouth shut."

"You won't get away with this," Harold said confidently. He knew by now that they weren't common criminals, probably some sort of twisted idealists. He didn't really fear them anymore. They were obviously sick individuals but they weren't killers. They could have killed him before now and no one would have been any the wiser.

"We'll see." Paul decided it wasn't worth the effort to continue this game. He had thought of taking the books and radio away but decided against it. It would all be over in a few days. One way or the other. He went out, slammed and bolted the door.

On Boxing Day the Woodsides had some of the neighbours in for a drink. During the hectic run-up to Christmas, Barbara Woodside had not had time to mull over the puzzling manner in which the Crowther's had left for their trip to America. But now that they were living on leftover turkey and mince pies she had an opportunity to indulge herself in speculation. In a corner of their over-stuffed lounge she went into a huddle with some of her friends who seemed equally intrigued by the situation as she outlined it.

"It does seem rather odd now that you mention it," one woman said. "It's not like Maura to disappear like that without saying a word to anyone."

"And remember," Barbara added, "Harold's own surgery didn't provide any enlightenment." She remembered Maura telling her that Harold had gone to a conference. It was passing strange that the surgery hadn't mentioned that. She added this nugget to the rising mound of curiosities. Her guests took all of it under advisement as they dipped into the dish of pretzels that Barbara passed around.

"You could call the airline and see if they were on board," another woman suggested.

"I tried that," Barbara said. "They don't give out that information. Let's just think about it. Did anyone notice anything strange in the days before they left? Anything out of the ordinary?"

An older woman started to say something but changed her mind.

"What is it?" Barbara pressed her.

"Well, I did see a youngish man go into the house fairly late one evening…"

"She's never having an affair…" someone else put in.

"Not Maura," Barbara said crossly. "Did he stay long in the house?"

"I wasn't paying much attention … Maybe fifteen minutes or so. He could have been anyone, a tradesman or insurance salesman. I thought at first he might have been delivering a telegram."

"A telegram?" Barbara repeated. "In this day and age? Come on, Tess." She didn't mean to be scathing but Tess took it badly.

"What do I know? What are you driving at anyway? Do you think Harold is buried under the cellar or what?"

"That's not so funny," Barbara riposted. Just then her husband joined them and inquired if they were being looked after all right. Even though he was three sheets in the wind he got the message that his solicitations were not appreciated at that moment. After he sloped off, the women resumed their discussion and Barbara finally announced that she would go to the police just to be on the safe side. There was general assent to this course of action.

The following day she presented herself at the local police station and spoke with the duty sergeant whom she knew slightly. He listened patiently to the rather complicated story and at the end of it asked a question which suggested that he hadn't really grasped the significance at all. Painstakingly, she went over it again. This time he did manage to grasp the essentials but pointed out – as she expected he would – that it was all conjecture and that there was no evidence to suggest that anything out of the ordinary had taken place. With a sinking feeling she realised that he was not the sort of thriller-writer's policeman who acted on the basis of hunch or instinct. It turned out that Harold was his dentist and had done some bridge work for him years ago, one result of which was that the sergeant had to give up pipe-smoking. He went on to explain how difficult it was to grip a pipe between teeth that had been weakened by dental intervention. But he hastened to point out that it was probably all for the best. Medically speaking.

At this stage when Barbara had given up, he floored her with a suggestion that at first seemed ludicrous.

"If you're that worried," he said, "Why don't you phone them up?"

"I don't know where they're staying in America," she said wearily.

"But the TV station that ran the quiz can give you that information," he said in his gentle lazy way.

She looked at him in amazement. "My god, you may have a point." She made for the door.

"Glad to be of service," he said to her departing back. The revolving door let in a blast of frozen air that played havoc with the coal fire. He made a mental note to get the door seals replaced.

CHAPTER 15

TWO DAYS BEFORE New Year's Eve they took the shuttle from La Guardia to Reagan Airport in Washington. The prize-winner guests filled the entire plane and the pilot gave them a special welcome, hoping they would enjoy the nation's capital at this interesting time. Earlier that morning Tim had told all and sundry that Reagan, formerly National, Airport was the most dangerous in the world because, being situated so centrally located – to accommodate politicians – it had very short runways and approach paths. In addition, planes landed and took off every minute, so it only took one pilot to make a slight error of judgement … The rest was ominously unsaid.

As they came in sight of Washington, Maura drew Patrick's attention to the sights which could be seen through the porthole. They followed the course of the Potomac and suddenly they could see the reflecting pool, the White House and the Capitol Building. With its neo-classical buildings, wide perspectives and a pervasive pearl-like colour, the city was more like Paris than New York. In the space of an hour they had come from what was perhaps the most lived-in, cosmopolitan city in the world to this designer-chic political cockpit. They circled the Washington Monument, coming so close that they could see the lightning conductor on top of the obelisk. Patrick's eyes were drawn elsewhere, to the War College at Green Leaf Point where Lincoln's assassin had been summarily hanged – and to Dumbarton Oaks where the UN had been founded. A wave of nausea passed through him, as if he were a captive brought in chains to ancient Rome to be humiliated before his execution.

A special coach met them just outside the Arrivals Lounge and brought them to their hotel, The Washington Towers, in Kalorama Triangle, not far from the area which housed most of the embassies. It was a magnificent hotel with the kind of cantilevered entrance and plush lobby that tend to be associated with major film premières. Glass elevators, shaped like torpedoes, rose and descended at every corner of the octagonal interior. Tim compared them to suppositories.

Art – still acting as den mother – told them something of the hotel's history, of the important treaties that had been signed in its various function rooms and of the many VIPs who stayed there while on government business. Tony Blair and George W. Bush had met there before going to the White House to plan the invasion of Iraq. Obama and Trump had used the hotel's facilities on more than one occasion. There were also, he added with a grin, several famous liaisons conducted within those walls, only a tiny proportion of which had ever been exposed by the press. He brought them to the Lincoln Room where the ball was to be held. It was, he said, the biggest function room in Washington. An army of engineers, designers, riggers and electricians were working on it around the clock, getting it ready for the big event.

"My god, it's spectacular," Maura said. She had never seen anything like it in her life. It wasn't just the scale but also the design, particularly, the mezzanine, and the furnishings which included many chandeliers, a semi-permanent stage and several grand pianos.

"Yes," Patrick agreed though he was looking at it through different eyes. He couldn't take it all in at that moment and would have to return as soon as possible.

"I wonder what our room will be like?" she mused aloud.

"I don't care ... just as long as you're there."

She kissed him and squeezed his hand. "Five minutes," she whispered.

They dismissed the busboy with an overgenerous tip and fell on each other, scattering clothes in all directions. They were almost naked by the time they reached the bedroom. There was some desperation about their love-making as if everything possible had to be compressed into the moment.

"I always thought I was ... sort of cold-blooded," she said later on.

"No, you're not."

"Not with you," she admitted.

"That's good. When people are in love it makes all the difference. It's natural…"

She knew he was right. This was no mere infatuation, but how on earth had she fallen in love with him so quickly against all the odds? It made no sense. She asked him if he was very experienced.

"No," he said with a smile. "But I suppose I had a good teacher…"

"Teacher?" It was Maura's turn to sit up and take stock.

He ran a hand through his hair. "I have a second cousin, Janine. We grew up together. She was always very curious about sex. Maybe she was a nymphomaniac, I'm not sure. She was three or four years older than me but she sort of picked on me for … experiments…"

"What sort of experiments? Wait now … Before you answer I'm going to order something from room service. I'm ravenous. How about you?"

"Good idea."

Maura picked up the phone from the bedside table and ordered a pot of coffee and a selection of club sandwiches.

"Now what about those experiments?"

"Oh, you know, she'd touch me in different places and ask me how it felt…"

"Was it abusive … I mean against your will?"

"I don't think so." He smiled. "We were pals really. And then she'd ask me to touch her and she'd give a running commentary. It was kind of funny. We used to go into a hay-shed to do it. I don't know if she learned much from me but I learned a lot from her…"

"Such as?" Maura was curious. In the space of little over a week he had gone – in her eyes – from a criminal to an uncompromising ideologue and now to an accomplished lover.

"Oh, you know…" He seemed reluctant to go into details; maybe he was even a little shy. Maura was amused by that. It wasn't as if he had to spare her blushes after what they'd just been through.

The waiter arrived with their order which they accepted in bed without any embarrassment though of course he didn't even turn a hair.

Patrick told her a little more about Janine. As she listened in silence Maura came to the conclusion that, by today's standards, Janine would almost certainly be regarded as an abuser. Patrick didn't seem to care.

"I don't think she did me any harm" he said with a grin.

When they finished eating he got up and went for a shower.

They sat around chatting for a good part of the morning and then he went to get his coat.

"Where are you going?" Maura asked him.

"I have to go out … for a while," he said

without further elaboration.

"I'll come with you … if you…"

"No, don't trouble yourself," he said, plainly ill-at-ease.

Her heart skipped a beat. She knew that he was getting down to business; the dream was coming to an end. It was sad and scary and there was nothing she could do about it. She didn't doubt his feelings for her but they didn't affect his sense of purpose in any way.

"I won't be long." He blew her a kiss from the door.

First he visited the Lincoln room which was still a hive of activity. He wandered at will among the workers, getting a feel for the layout. He noted where the stage was being completed and the position of the doors that led on to it. There was a balcony that ran around three sides of the hall; two staircases led up to it, one of them quite close to the main entrance. There were two other entrances and three fire doors. He committed it all to memory, then left the hotel and hailed a cab.

He crossed the river to Virginia and went to a shopping mall about five miles to the south of McLean. He paid off the cab after he found the store that Paul had described to him. He went in and browsed until the last customer had left.

Then he approached the counter.

"And what may I interest you in today, sir?" the gunsmith inquired with a smile.

"Could I see some hand-guns?" Patrick asked. This was part of Plan B – in case he couldn't get close enough to Dwyer with the syringe. He had thought of a rifle; one corner of the mezzanine would have been a perfect spot but he reckoned that there would be absolutely no way he could smuggle in a rifle on the night. And the possibility of concealing it somewhere in the hall beforehand was too risky since it would probably be discovered by one of the workmen – or in the course of a security sweep.

The man opened a case behind the counter and showed Patrick a selection of side arms, Berettas, Walthers and Remingtons. Patrick was about to opt for one of the smaller Berettas – in fact any of them would suit – when he chanced to see a Kaltronic .38 in another case close to a rack of hunting rifles. The irony was compelling. He nodded towards it.

As the man brought it out he said, "Top of the range but it doesn't come cheap."

Patrick tested the magazine and trigger-pull and said he'd take it as well as a box of medium-powder loads.

The man asked to see his licence. Without looking at him, Patrick produced a hundred dollar bill and placed it on the counter. The man demurred. Patrick had a bad moment, wondering if the intelligence provided by Paul had been defective. Without flinching, he laid another large denomination bill on the counter – part of the proceeds of the bank robbery.

"Want to test it?" the man asked, slipping the two bills into his pocket.

Patrick nodded. They went down a narrow staircase at the back of the shop and into a bare stone room with a bank of sandbags and targets at one end. Disdaining ear muffs, Patrick loaded the weapon and fired a few rounds, adapting himself to the stronger than expected recoil, until he found the centre of the target. He pronounced himself satisfied.

When they went back upstairs the man asked with studied casualness whether he wanted a silencer. Patrick shook his head; he had considered that earlier and felt that it would serve no useful purpose in the circumstances. If the syringe didn't work and he had to fall back on the gun, it really wasn't going to make any difference to his survival whether he used a silencer or not. He paid in cash, picked up the package and left.

He took a cab back to DC and as they passed along Constitution Avenue he saw monuments to past Presidents at every hand's turn. Had they been so noble, heroic and motivated by public service as their statues proclaimed? If so what had happened in more recent years, in his generation? How could it all have gone so badly wrong? In one sense the answer was fairly simple: after a given period of time was it not inevitable that great powers would become corrupted? Had there ever been a single exception to that rule in all of history? Putting these thoughts aside, he asked the driver to stop at a florist's where he picked up a dozen roses.

Maura was in the bath when he presented them to her. She reached up to him and he reached down to her.

CHAPTER 16

IT SEEMED ALMOST perverse that New Year's Eve arrived in the same grey blustery garb as any other winter day. The management of the hotel drew a collective sigh of relief as the workmen finally gathered up their tools and surplus materials and left the Lincoln Room, which was transformed. But no sooner had they left than an army of security men invaded the hall to do a final sweep and decide on strategic positions.

They were coordinated by Frank Corcoran, an experienced FBI agent. He had spent the last two weeks listening to the advice and demands of different Federal Agencies and of KNYBS, but the final decisions lay with him. He had a clean record to date and he wasn't about to let anything sully that. Although the President of the US would not be attending this function, Corcoran decided to proceed as if he were; in other words he was assigning maximum priority to the security arrangements. He didn't like the air of madness that often surrounded the end of the year. When people started acting differently it could cause a chain reaction with consequences that were entirely unpredictable. There were a lot of loony-tunes just waiting for an opportunity to come out of the woodwork. Corcoran decided this would not happen; not on his watch.

Maura and Patrick sat in the dining room having a light breakfast. Both were absorbed in their own thoughts. She eventually broke the silence, "I can't believe it's come at last." She wanted to say more – about time running out, but the O'Malleys were seated quite close to them.

Patrick looked closely at her, "Are you all right?"

"I'm OK."

They made their way with the other guests to a function room on the second floor where Art briefed them on the arrangements and protocol for the party that evening. He distributed programmes which he went over with them. The musicians and entertainers would arrive sometime in the afternoon. It would take them a couple of hours to set up. At nine o'clock the hosts would form a receiving line in the Lincoln Room. All going well, the VIP guests would arrive during the following half hour or so, after which the prize-winners would make their entrance.

"So we're just the riff raff," someone said to Art, half in earnest, half in jest.

"Not at all," he replied stoutly. "It's just that you all know each other at this stage. So it's better that you go in together. It will help to break down barriers."

"We believe you, Art," another voice piped up to the accompaniment of laughter.

"Well, I hope you have a great time," he said, mollified. "And if there's anything you need, you know where I am."

Bob Carraway had flown to Washington on the 30th December to check on the arrangements for the ball. The executives of KNYBS had given him a full briefing. The next afternoon he met Lawrence at Reagan Airport and both men spent some time in the VIP Lounge. Bob told Lawrence that everything was in a state of readiness and that the guest list looked like something out of the Marquis 'Who's Who in the World'. The response to the invitations had been remarkable, especially in view of the fact that several other glitzy parties were planned up and down the east coast.

"That's great," Lawrence said, trying to share his enthusiasm. It didn't matter to him if only a handful of people turned up just as long as Evelyn was going to be there. He longed for the day when Kaltronics had such a dominant market position that PR was no longer required.

"And what's more," Bob went on, "KNYBS tell me their ratings have gone up already. Imagine what they'll be like afterwards."

"Are they filming the event tonight?" Lawrence hadn't had time to check this out beforehand.

"They'll have cameras in the lobby of the hotel," Bob said, "To interview celebrities on the way in…"

"But not inside?"

"No … if that's all right with you…"

"That's fine." Lawrence was relieved.

"We reckoned that having cameras in the Lincoln Room might be … em … inhibiting. I imagine people are going to let their hair down as the witching hour approaches." He laughed a little nervously. The success or otherwise of the event rested squarely on his shoulders – and success would be defined largely in terms of Lawrence's opinion. He had warned reporters not to buttonhole Lawrence under any circumstances. There was of course always the risk that some snot-nosed cub or paparazzo would pop out of the woodwork, but Bob had done all in his power to minimise that risk, by calling in favours far and wide. He knew that while Lawrence was prepared to say a few words on stage, it meant precisely that. So he had slotted him into the schedule for one minute and no more.

In the last week as the hacks were beating the bushes, Bob had gotten wind of a piece being written about the connection between KNYBS and Kaltronics. The journalist had apparently unearthed some hard evidence which would be difficult to refute. Bob managed to get it spiked but he now owed the editor big time and they both knew it.

They went by limousine to guest quarters on Pennsylvania Avenue. After Lawrence unpacked his overnight bag, Bob offered him a drink which was declined.

"If you want anything to eat," Bob said, "there's a housekeeper in the kitchen and…"

"I had something on the plane, thanks."

"If you'd like to nap you won't be disturbed."

"I've got some work to do." Lawrence tapped his brief case. "Don't worry about me. I'll be just fine. You probably want to go over to the hotel."

"As a matter of fact, I do. Last minute checks … You're sure you'll be all right …?"

"Go. Go," Lawrence said. "I'll see you later."

After Bob left he got down to some work but he didn't concentrate very well. Evelyn seemed to be waiting in the wings of his mind, about to make an entrance. At six o'clock he tidied his papers away, showered and changed into his dress suit.

"You're sure you don't want me to go to West Virginia?" Evelyn asked Stanley as the valet packed his bags. She was on firm ground asking that question – and she knew it.

"No. That's all right," Stanley replied.

"You're expected at the ball. Besides, I've some Congressmen to cajole – or whip into line. It would bore you to tears. Hell, it's going to bore the pants off me too, but I can't get out of it."

"You're not going to be working all night?" she asked in a tone of almost genuine sympathy.

"Oh, I imagine we'll manage a little celebration later on, hum a bar or two of 'Auld Lang Syne'. It might even oil the wheels of compromise." He was reasonably sure that he would be able to get enough support for his budgetary proposals. William shared his confidence.

It occurred to her that Lawrence was probably already in town. Finally – and to her great relief – an aide called to collect the bags and Stanley left with him.

Before going for her shower Evelyn appraised her naked body in a full length mirror. She had kept her figure remarkably well, helped by a nip and tuck two years earlier. Her daily exercise routine – a form of Pilates which concentrated on tummy and thighs – had also proved its worth. She felt pleased with herself, rang for her hairdresser and told her to come to her room in fifteen minutes.

Lillian Bartok and her young lover, Boyd, had spent most of the morning in bed together in her Georgetown apartment. He was indefatigable and as he reached for her again she gently and reluctantly pushed him away.

"I have to get up," she sighed. "Have to get ready for the ball. Who am I, Cinderella?"

"Now that you've had your wicked way with me you're kicking me out of bed," Boyd said with mock petulance. "And I guess I'm not invited to this bash either."

"You know how it is, lover. You'd be bored out of your skull anyway." She gave him a passing kiss on the cheek and made to get up.

"You're ashamed to be seen with me in public." He continued the parody with trembling under-lip. "You only want me for my body."

"Hey, studmeister, there are other fish in the sea. And you're getting a little paunchy." She patted his belly and let her hand slip down to his groin. "Seriously though, it's a command performance and it's also work, at least for me. You don't mind, do you?"

"No," he said. "It's not my scene. I'd probably drink too much and throw up over the glitterati."

At least, she thought, he didn't say he'd have nothing in common with all those old fogeys. Age was more of an issue for her than for him. What had started out as a purely physical relationship was, from her standpoint, turning into something more, and it worried her. She was on a hiding to nothing. The day would come when he would meet someone his own age and that would be that. She would fall out of the sky in a trail of smoke like a discarded booster rocket, and he would continue to soar.

"Is our beloved Congressman Ralston going?" he asked.

"No. But his wife Evelyn is. I'm sort of chaperoning her."

"I'm impressed."

She watched him as he hopped into his tight-fitting jeans. She liked to look at his hard, lean body. Life-drawing had been a hobby of hers seven or eight years ago, and she found the young male body far more challenging than the female, with its many tight knots of muscle as opposed to smooth curves.

"Catch you later," he said.

"You're a darling."

"Missing you already," he sang out as he started down the stairs.

She knew that he would probably go to some student party and she also realised with a pang that she would have no place there. They belonged to different orbits which didn't intersect.

She recovered her spirits when Evelyn's driver arrived to pick her up.

CHAPTER 17

EVELYN'S ADC STAYED in the background as she and Lillian got out of the car and braved the battery of photographers and reporters who thronged the hotel entrance. Evelyn wore a full length *crêpe de chine* dress that took on a silver sheen every time a flashbulb popped. Lillian followed behind in a duster coat and wrap sarong skirt. The police and security men made a path for them while the aide fended off questions from the enthusiastic journalists who threatened to set foot on the red carpet.

Once inside the lobby they were taken in hand by Bob and the senior hotel manager. Bob asked her if she would mind saying a few words to the KNYBS reporter who stood in front of the camera crew. They were harmless apolitical questions. Yes, she was looking forward to the evening and hoped everyone would have a good time. Yes, she hoped the next year would be one of peace around the world. No, unfortunately her husband couldn't make it, much as he wanted to; pressure of work, believe it or not.

They were brought directly to a suite on the fourth floor where they could relax before the function began.

"We're delighted you could attend," Bob said unctuously. "And we would be honoured if you would join us in the receiving line at 9 o'clock in the Lincoln Room."

"Has Lawrence Dwyer arrived yet?"

"No, Ma'am. But he's expected shortly."

With a flourish the manager pointed out the refreshments that had been laid on.

"We'll be just fine," Evelyn said.

Bob and the manager withdrew and the aide took up a position outside the door.

Lillian poured two glasses of champagne and handed one to Evelyn. "Drink up, girl. It's going to be a long night. Do you remember the last time we talked?"

"Yes. That theory of yours."

"It's becoming less theoretical as time passes," Lillian said. "Have you had an opportunity of discussing it with Stanley?"

"Yes, but I didn't get very far. He wasn't too … forthcoming." Lillian really was single-minded, Evelyn thought, bringing this up now of all times.

"Hmmm."

"What does that mean?"

"Well, look Evelyn, we've been exchanging confidences for years now and you know that I know how … what shall I say …? tepid your relationship with Stanley is. I mean it's hardly…"

"Don't beat about the bush," Evelyn said. "What are you driving at?"

"I think you might have more influence with Lawrence. He'd listen to you." Lillian got up and paced, straightening out the folds of her sarong skirt.

"I'm not so sure about that," Evelyn demurred. "Why would he listen to me?"

"Because he always did … Take him to bed if you have to."

"Oh, come on." Evelyn said disparagingly, although that particular thought wasn't far from her mind.

"What I mean is, cultivate him. There was always a special bond between you two. You know, the yin and yang. You could make him see sense. I'm sure of it. Anyway," Lillian continued, "I'm not going to labour the point. Just think about it. That's all I ask."

Evelyn nodded, then laid down her glass. "God, the end of another year. The years are beginning to slip by so quickly now. There's something scary about it. Still, it's not the end of the world, I suppose."

"Could be the end of the world as we know it," Lillian said, "if this 'Pox Americana' comes to fruition. I imagine that a hundred and twenty years ago people were celebrating the *fin de siècle* and looking forward to a brave new world. And what did they get? World wars on a massive scale … That's why you have to talk to Dwyer. Sorry to harp on it again. But he's … well, I have to say it … a fascist."

"No," Evelyn said. "You don't understand him. He wouldn't even know what you mean by that. He just goes for things. That's his nature. Maybe he's a little short in the imagination department. There's certainly no ideology involved. I can guarantee that."

"Why does he shun publicity so much? We've tried to interview him dozens of times. Unsuccessfully, I might add."

"That's just not his thing," Evelyn said loyally.

"Are you saying he's shy?" Lillian gave a peal of incredulous laughter. She re-filled her glass and when Evelyn declined, replaced the bottle in the ice bucket on the credenza.

"What's so strange about that?"

"Christ, he's just trying to avoid responsibility. You must really be smitten. Where's your critical faculty?"

"That's not fair."

"Sorry. I know it's not fair." Lillian gazed into the middle distance. She knew how Evelyn and Lawrence were split up when they were in their twenties. And she knew from her own experience how the heart could be too forgiving. It was entirely possible that she herself had become hard-bitten and cynical over the years. On the other hand she had rarely, if ever, met anyone in a position of power – including ecclesiastics – who acted selflessly in pursuit of the greater good. She drained her glass.

Evelyn glanced at her watch. "It's time to go down."

"Another few minutes. Ladies should never

be on time."

They went to the bathroom to make minor adjustments to hair and make-up.

"We're still too fine fillies," Lillian said, looking into the mirror. "OK, let's go and kick ass." She displayed her strong American teeth.

Lawrence stood awkwardly in the receiving line with Bob and several other dignitaries, including the President of KNYBS. A toastmaster made the introductions as the invitees entered and he also acquitted himself well in the skillful task of allowing each guest adequate opportunity to chat to the hosts while at the same time ensuring that the later guests did not have to stand in line for too long. The early arrivals were reasonably well spaced, however, so Lawrence had a chance to talk to two Senators, three Congressmen, a well-known Broadway actor and their respective wives – all in formal attire.

"Damn good idea, this bash," an elderly British General was saying to Lawrence. "Helps the special relationship between Britain and the US. We can still teach you a thing or two."

"I'm sure you can," Lawrence said with a smile.

"Of course, old man. Remember, we were

on the winning side twice. You chaps took a bit of a bashing in Vietnam. Still, you did all right in Iraq. Have to give you that. Where's the booze?"

"Mind your liver, dear," his wife warned him. They walked towards the nearest buffet table, the General's medals rattling on his chest.

And still they came, stars of stage and screen, captains of industry, literati, church leaders. Many of them had already been interviewed by the TV crew in the lobby and were in a highly voluble state, as if there was much more they'd wanted to say to camera. The toastmaster was put to the pin of his collar to keep the line moving.

During one short lull Lawrence said to Bob, "I'm not sure I can take much more." He had pains in his calf muscles and was running out of small talk, his repertoire of which was not plentiful to start with.

"It won't take much longer," Bob assured him.

Lawrence saw Evelyn before she saw him. He stepped forward without thinking and embraced her. She took her place in the receiving line and introduced Lillian, who diplomatically excused herself and made for the champagne.

"It's great to see you again," Lawrence said. "You look wonderful." His eyes lingered over her.

"I can return the compliment." She smiled

and stood beside him, welcoming guests who now came thick and fast, including a group of French billionaires who had left Paris some seven hours earlier in an executive jet. Between the kow-towing and the chit-chat Lawrence and Evelyn managed to exchange glances but little else. At the far end of the vast hall a twenty-piece orchestra began to tune up while engineers tested the sound systems.

Maura and Patrick sat in the lobby watching the proceedings. They wore ID tags which Art had distributed to the prize-winners that afternoon. They could see into the Lincoln Room and, through the revolving doors of the hotel, they could also see the big cars pull up and the celebrities glide across the red carpet under the cantilevered entrance. If they hadn't been so tense they might have been amused at the way in which celebrities so quickly donned exuberant expressions when the cameras were turned on them. All of the arrivals had to go through a security check just inside the entrance. The security staff seemed to have been trained at charm school for dealing with prima donnas.

The only awkward incident was when a party who had travelled over on the QE2 cut up a little rough. Some of them were drunk, having spent five days on a rough sea. They were politely ushered to a private suite where they were given strong black coffee.

Because of his pre-assigned identity tag,

Patrick didn't have to go through security. Through the open doors of the Lincoln Room he caught occasional glimpses of Lawrence Dwyer in the receiving line. He had a plan of sorts but nothing definite. There were many variables beyond his control, so a degree of flexibility was necessary. One of the major unknowns was how long Dwyer would stay at the ball. It was possible that he would leave before midnight. Following his movements in such a large, crowded hall was also going to be difficult.

Patrick tried as best he could to pick out the bodyguards, private security men and members of the Executive Protection Unit which was part of the Secret Service. Those with the ear pieces and talking cuffs were easy enough to detect but he was sure there were dozens of others posing as guests and waiters. There seemed to be a disproportionate number of single men on that part of the mezzanine which he could see. He felt sure that FBI agents were also present. Instinctively, he patted his breast pocket and felt the outline of the spectacles. The .38 was tucked into the back of his waistband, hidden by the jacket.

Maura eyed the passing parade with a mixture of excitement and fear. Occasionally, the sight of major celebrities gave her a sense of reassurance as if nothing bad could happen in the midst of such high-profile people; they exuded a sort of natural inviolability. The laughter, however phoney, was infectious, and the insouciance of some of her screen idols tended to rub off on her. It was real but dream-like at the same time. The fact that she was only one of two people out of thousands who knew it could turn into a nightmare somehow lessened the effect of that knowledge. She slipped in and out of denial.

Because of the ambient noise Patrick didn't hear the name 'Harold Crowther' being called out over the public address system. Neither did anyone else. Probably sensing that this was the case, a manager of the hotel resorted to a more old-fashioned paging system. He sent a bus boy around the lobby with a placard bearing the name in magic marker. Tim O'Malley was the first to see it. He quizzed the bus boy and told him to leave it to him. He rushed across the lobby and clapped a hand on Patrick's shoulder.

"Harold, there's a message for you."

Patrick jumped. "What?"

"A phone call for you at reception."

"Who?" Patrick asked. His mind lurched into overdrive. If it was Paul it could only mean one thing: abort the plan. He half-hoped that would be the case. But he had spoken to Paul only two days ago …

"Someone from England. Barbara Woodshaw, I think."

Maura looked up in alarm. "Woodside?"

"Yes. That's it." Tim looked from one of them to the other. "Woodside … I hope …

everything is all right."

"I'm sure it is." Patrick got up and walked over to the reception desk, trying to appear casual, though his pulse rate had shot up; he was so preoccupied that he passed right in front of the TV cameras.

CHAPTER 18

STANLEY STROLLED WITH William in the woods near his retreat in West Virginia. Most of the business had been completed and they were taking a breather before their modest celebration got under way.

"I think you've got those mavericks sorted out," William said, referring to the Congressmen who had previously taken a rather jaundiced view of his Budget proposals.

"I hope so." Stanley chuckled softly. "I think they realised we meant business when we dragged them up here on New Year's Eve." In a gleam of moonlight he saw a squirrel dart up the trunk of a tree and chase through the bare branches.

"It's also a vote of confidence in you," William pointed out. "They wouldn't have been quite so biddable unless they were pretty sure about your second term. They know which side their bread is buttered on."

"Well, the polls aren't exactly encouraging."

"Not yet. But it's only a question of time and effort. The Congressmen are aware of the strong reputation CASA has. And they know the kind of resources your campaign will have." With the toe of his shoe William flicked a stone into the lake and watched the ripples spread out.

"According to my calculations we only need to keep seven of our ducks in a row for our Budget proposals to go through, assuming the White House buys the package. But," he held up a forefinger, "that will only be the beginning. We'll need a big publicity campaign to get the message across that world peace is the issue, that America must not shrink from her responsibilities, that sort of thing."

"Peace enforcing…"

"We shouldn't put it like that. It could be misconstrued."

"You're right. I can handle the publicity. It's a matter of selling the concept."

"That's right."

"And we have a war chest for that," William said.

"Break it out. Now is the time."

William paused and thought for a while. "I wonder if it would be better to keep the Budgetary proposals under wraps until after your second term begins. It might take time to mould public opinion. That caucus of liberal snowflakes on the Hill can be quite vociferous. Time is on our side."

"Maybe you're right," Stanley conceded. "It'll take a while to explain these issues to the public, to put the proper spin on them." He trusted William's judgement. With anyone else he would look for the hidden agenda, the self-serving angle.

"There could be misunderstandings," William continued. "You know, close ties with the arms industry. That sort of thing."

"Right. We must avoid that elephant trap."

"Wrong impressions…"

"That's right."

They walked on a wooden jetty that led to a small marina on the lake. It was deserted; all of the boats were in dry dock. They startled a blue heron that flapped out of the water and disappeared into the mist.

"I wonder if it's a good idea to depend to such an extent on Lawrence Dwyer's support. We need him of course but he shouldn't think he's indispensable."

Stanley nodded. "I think you have a point." He didn't elaborate further.

When they reached the end of the pier they stopped, faced each other, embraced and kissed.

Stanley was the first to decouple and he did so with reluctance. "We have to be more careful than ever, Bill," he said.

"I know it." William replied sadly.

"Are you sure you're all right?" Tim asked, staring into Maura's pale face.

"Yes. It's just … you know … a phone call out of the blue." Barbara Woodside, she thought, that busybody, always sticking her nose in … Maura's loyalties were so divided she didn't know which side she was on any more. Or were there sides?

Tim sat down beside her. "It's probably nothing … Would you like a drink or maybe …?"

"No thank you."

As Patrick approached the reception desk he knew he would have to take the call if only because he was in Tim O'Malley's line of sight. The fact that he had mistakenly walked in front of the TV cameras unnerved him. This Barbara Woodside must be a friend of the Crowthers; he had inferred that much from Maura's reaction. Slowly he picked up the receiver and put it to his ear, not really knowing how he was going to handle the situation.

"Harold? Is that you, Harold? It's Barbara here…"

He thought quickly. There was no way he could mimic Harold's voice in a way that would pass muster with a neighbour. "No," he said. "But I'm a friend of his…"

"And he's there with you … and Maura is also there?"

"Oh, yes. Maura too. They're both here. But I think they have already gone to the party. Can I give them a message?"

"Well, I'm Barbara Woodside. I … we were worried about them … I tried Maura's phone, but couldn't get through…"

"They're fine … I'll tell them you called."

After a slight pause she said, "Could you ask them to call me as soon as they can?"

"Of course. Certainly."

"Who am I speaking to?"

"Jacques … Montret. I will ask them to call you."

"Thank you."

As he walked back towards Maura he wondered if the caller had bought that. It probably didn't matter one way or the other. There was less than a few hours to go.

"Well?" Maura inquired.

"It was nothing," he said. "The Woodsides just wanted to wish us a happy New Year."

"There, I told you," Tim said. "Nothing to worry about." He got up. "I'd better go and see if Clare has finished beautifying herself yet."

When he was out of earshot Maura asked what it was really about.

"I'm not sure," Patrick said. "I think they were worried about the way you disappeared. I told her you or Harold would call back."

Maura made no response for a while. Then she grasped his arm and said in an urgent whisper, "Listen to me, Patrick, you can walk away from this … this, whatever it is. It's not too late. You could leave right now … I'll go with you if you like … I want Harold to be freed, but I won't identify you … or let you down. You can still opt out of this. Please…"

"I can't." He shook his head slowly. "If it … goes badly … you must leave. Go home.

You're not involved…"

His words cut her to the quick and it took a great effort on her part to stem the tears that began to well in her eyes.

Eventually they went into the Lincoln Room. The toastmaster was replaced by Art, who made the introductions, and no one in the receiving line paid them any great attention. Bob gave them his fixed smile and robotic handshake. Maura saw how Patrick looked at Dwyer; there was a calculation in his eyes she had not seen before. Evelyn expressed the hope that they would enjoy themselves, but even as she spoke she looked over their heads at the guests coming behind.

They gravitated to one of the buffet tables, behind which stood a phalanx of chefs and waiters. The variety of the hot and cold dishes was astonishing. The 'raw bar' alone offered oysters, mussels, wild and smoked salmon, king prawns and Maine lobster. To the left of the bandstand there was a giant screen and to the right, rising above the mezzanine, was a rocket capsule donated by the Smithsonian. Many couples were already on the floor dancing.

"How're you folks?" a cheery American couple greeted them as they came off the dancing area.

"We're very well, thank you," Patrick said. Maura added a pleasantry. The man introduced himself and his wife.

"You sound British," he said.

"Yes"

"Ted is the Governor of Maryland," the woman said. "What is it that you do? Not politics, I hope."

"No," Maura answered. "Dentistry."

"You're a dentist?" the woman inquired.

"No, my husband is. We're prize-winners."

The American couple soon wandered off. There was something disdainful about the movement of the woman's shoulder-blades in her backless dress. The O'Malleys had witnessed the scene.

"We've just had the same treatment," Clare O'Malley said. "You'd think we were lepers. And Americans always boast about being classless."

"But the class system over here isn't based on birth," Tim explained. "It's a question of what you've achieved. As prize-winners we're just lucky. We haven't achieved anything. Not as they see it."

"But isn't it supposed to be a republic?" Patrick put in. "Things of the people."

"It doesn't mean that everyone has an equal voice," Tim said. "Far from it. Remember the streets of New York? The bag-ladies and panhandlers?"

"Strange how everything changes ... mutates," Patrick said, almost to himself. "Even socialism gives way to elites. It doesn't say much for human nature."

"Original sin," Clare said. "What do you

think, Maura?"

"I suppose so. The common denominator is greed. No system can change that." She saw that Patrick was nodding.

"Well, we prize-winners should enjoy it while we have it," Clare tried to lighten the conversation. "In a couple of days we're going to be busted back to the ranks. Why don't we sample the goodies while we have the chance?"

They went to one of the buffets and brought their plates to a table near the back of the hall. It was apparent that the best tables had been reserved for the celebrities. Still, there were no further complaints as they enjoyed the superb cuisine. Maura could only pick at her food, however, and Clare remarked on this. Tim came to the rescue by explaining the fright she had received earlier due to the unexpected phone call.

"People can be so inconsiderate," Clare said, referring to Barbara Woodside, "Though of course they probably mean well. But look, we're here now on this marvellous occasion. Let's make the most of it." She raised her glass. "I'd like to propose a toast. To new and absent friends."

They drank to that and so did a party of fellow prize-winners at a neighbouring table.

"Did you notice the balloons?" one of them asked, pointing upwards.

They all looked up to see hundreds of multi-coloured balloons held in a huge net suspended from the ceiling. They would be released no doubt at the stroke of midnight.

"You can't beat the Americans for razzmatazz," Tim opined.

"Shock and awe," Patrick added. It wasn't clear whether he was agreeing or not.

Tim consulted the programme and reminded the others of what was in store. After the buffet and dancing there would be a retrospective pageant on the big screen. Then between ten and eleven, items symbolising the year's events would be placed in the Smithsonian time capsule which would later be buried in a vault near Mount Vernon. Dancing would recommence and continue until 11.55 p.m., after which the countdown would begin. After the turn of the year the party would start all over again and continue into the wee hours. There would be several side-shows, including a fireworks display in the hotel grounds.

Patrick excused himself and reconnoitred the hall. He was relieved when he finally located Lawrence Dwyer. Predictably enough he was seated at one of the reserved tables close to the stage. The main uncertainty still related to how long he was going to stay. He wasn't mentioned at all in the programme so it was conceivable that he could leave at any time. Patrick had to take a risk; he found one of the hotel managers and asked him who would be introducing the different events set out in the programme.

"The Chairman of KNYBS will introduce most of them," the manager said.

"I was hoping to hear Mr. Dwyer," Patrick said. "I'm a great admirer of his."

"I'm afraid he won't be making a speech."

"That's too bad. I was also hoping to have a word with him on a business matter but I wouldn't wish to interrupt him." Patrick nodded in the direction of the VIP table. "You wouldn't by any chance happen to know when he is planning to leave? I could perhaps catch him then."

"I don't know exactly, sir. But I think he'll be here till midnight."

"Oh?"

"He has kindly agreed to do the countdown. But that should take less than a minute."

"Thank you for your help," Patrick said. It wasn't as reassuring as he would have liked but it was better than nothing. He assumed that the logical place to do the countdown was the podium in front of the bandstand.

Shortly after Patrick walked away agent Frank Corcoran approached the manager.

"What did that guy want?"

"He was just inquiring about the speeches."

"Who is he?" Corcoran pressed.

"One of the guests, sir."

"Tell me something I don't know," Corcoran said roughly.

"He's one of the KNYBS prize-winners … from England, I believe."

"Is he on his own?"

"No, sir. His wife is with him."

Corcoran filed away the information and beckoned to one of his men who was dressed as a waiter.

At the VIP table Bob told Evelyn how much he admired the work she did with public-school kids.

"You're very kind. But I'm not sure what impact any of us can have. The drug situation is becoming an epidemic. I don't know how we can stem the tide, and the consequences are appalling. A new underclass is emerging. Youngsters are using assault weapons and committing awful crimes. There are drive-by shootings almost every day. And many of these crimes do seem to be related to drugs, especially crack cocaine." She dabbed the side of her mouth delicately with a linen napkin.

"They've recently put some of the dealers in the Marines and made men of them," Bob said. "They had a fairly good success rate with that." He refilled her glass with sparkling hock and watched how she sipped it, her everted lips barely touching the glass.

"I'm not so sure." Lillian bought into the conversation. "Revolving door justice perpetuates it. There are no real sanctions anymore."

"Tell that to the guys on death row," Bob said, a little more forcefully then he'd intended.

"I wish there was more the media could do about it," one of the KNYBS executives said with a faint sigh. "But we have a dilemma. The more we highlight the problem the greater the risk that even younger kids will want to experiment with drugs. It's a double-edged sword."

A populist Senator intervened, "Hey guys, it's New Year's Eve."

"I don't agree with that." As a professional journalist, Lillian was keen to assert her viewpoint. "It depends on how the material is handled. It seems to me that television, in particular, portrays the drug user as an anti-hero and that has a perverse appeal for many youngsters who see themselves as victims. The reality is that drug use is a form of weakness and it should be depicted as such."

Evelyn sneaked a look at Lawrence to see how he was taking all this. He met her glance and smiled.

"I think you're over-simplifying, Lillian", the KNYBS man said. "It really isn't as easy as that. The format of documentaries is a secondary issue. The fact is that for one reason or another there are a great many young people in this country who are self-destructive or suicidal. We can't even hope to deal with this epidemic – as Evelyn rightly calls it – without going into the roots of this culture … It's not just a matter of social deprivation but also a sense of exclusion…"

"There's one way you could stop it spreading," Lawrence said.

"And what's that?" Lillian asked abruptly.

"Make drugs legal. Let the addicts have their fixes at the going market rate, under medical supervision. Prices would collapse, the pushers and dealers would go out of business. The muggings and murders would stop."

"Oh now," Lillian demurred. "The free market can't solve this." She was damned if she'd agree with Dwyer. "The free market brought us all those toxic financial products back in 2008…"

"But it *can* solve it," Lawrence said lightly.

"What you're really saying," she persisted "is that addicts are beyond help … So you provide them with cheap drugs and let them kill themselves."

"No. They can always quit." He tapped his temple. "Free will."

"Hardly, if they're addicted," Lillian insisted.

"Look," Lawrence said, "that's an admirable liberal viewpoint. But who made them addicts in the first place? And don't say 'society'. Who stops them from quitting? They've even got methadone programmes for god's sake. No. Give them the stuff on demand and get them off the streets. Problem solved."

"I think Lawrence is on to something very important here." Bob added his fawning two cents worth.

"No government would have the guts to do it," Evelyn pointed out.

"You should know," Lillian said.

"Hey, guys," the senator said from further down the table. "Party time … Chill pills all round."

"Look," Lawrence said, ignoring the senator's plea, "It's often the parents' fault…"

"That's outrageous," Lillian cut in. And, without quite knowing why, she added that he probably believed in conversion therapy for gays.

"Relevance, Your Honour?" Lawrence inquired lightly.

"But you're not denying it," she pressed.

"I'm not discussing it," he said.

"Because you're afraid of being accused of hate speech."

"Miss Bartok, you may believe in political correctness, but I do not. It does not mean you have the moral high ground. It's just a difference of opinion…"

"No, no … absolutely not…" Lillian began. But then Evelyn dealt herself a hand by dragging Lawrence away from the table onto the dance floor. Making it seem as if she were defusing a situation was good cover. Suddenly she was in his arms, close to him, feeling protected. The years fell away.

"It's been a while." She smiled up at him.

"Too long."

"We used to dance like this years ago."

"I remember."

She could remember how he took the corners in rather jerky movements; he was not a graceful dancer by any means. But being close to him again was the touchstone of a long-cherished dream. Although there were no professional photographers in the room they had to be careful of prying eyes and phones. While in the receiving line she reckoned that up to a quarter of the guests were politicians, most of them known to her and Stanley.

Patrick noticed with alarm that Dwyer was no longer seated at the VIP table. He asked Maura to dance and she agreed with some reluctance. The floor was very crowded and he became more and more uneasy until, eventually, he caught a glimpse of Dwyer walking his partner back to the table and sitting beside her. At one point Maura's hand slipped down his back and she felt the gun in his waistband.

"Oh, Christ … Patrick." She froze.

"Ignore it," he said. "Forget about it."

"How can I?" She went back to the table and he followed her. Fortunately the O'Malleys were out dancing. After a long silence Patrick opened his mouth to say something but changed his mind. Everything had already been said and the wheels were in motion; further talk now would be stupid and dangerous. Besides, he had no words to calm Maura's fears.

She went to the Ladies where she promptly got sick. She looked at her face in the mirror; it was hard to believe that she was involved in this. Where was the rewind button that would allow her to go back to her comfortable, even-keel existence in Hertingfordbury before any of this began? Should she at least warn Dwyer? How could she stand idly by and let a man be killed? Yet if she somehow managed to warn him what would befall Patrick? This was America; if he showed any resistance at all they would shoot him on the spot and ask questions later. And he would resist. She knew him. It was Dwyer's life or his.

"Cheer up." A woman stood beside her opening a compact. "It might never happen."

"Right." Maura forced a washed-out smile. Unfortunately, she knew better: something awful was going to happen.

Patrick kept his eyes on Dwyer and noticed how he monopolised the woman he was with – or was it the other way around? He was fairly sure by now that he could identify at least two of Dwyer's bodyguards. The official security men, even those in waiter's uniforms, were conspicuous enough. So too were the White House aides. He reckoned that there were probably dozens more at strategic places in the hall and mezzanine.

"All on your own?" One of the German

guests inquired.

"For the moment," Patrick said.

"Well, I'm not going to ask you to dance." The man roared with laughter at his own joke.

The O'Malleys returned breathless from the dance floor to the table where Clare drank copious quantities of iced water.

"Oh, that's better. It's hard work out there."

"Ta very much," Tim said drily, pulling out a chair for Maura who had just returned.

"Some of these celebs can't dance at all," Clare observed. "You'd be amazed."

"They don't make so many musicals anymore," Tim said. "You don't have to sing or dance to be a star nowadays." He took a long pull at his beer, a beverage chosen to pace himself until the action really got going.

"Maybe there's hope for you then." Clare said.

"Maybe I'm already a star…"

A drum roll silenced them. Bob, who had been waiting in the wings, walked on stage towards the microphone, welcomed everyone and said that the next half hour or so would be devoted to a screen-based pageant based on the significant events of the year about to expire.

"This better be good," Tim whispered. "We've been bombarded by retrospectives already."

Bob introduced a well-known KNYBS anchorman who would do the narration.

"It's a wonder they haven't got a gospel

choir," Clare remarked.

There followed an unorthodox presentation of recent history. Every event seemed to revolve around the US, and the anchorman's script seemed to have been jointly written by Professor Pangloss and Pollyanna .

It started in a light-hearted manner about the Oscar awards that year which suggested that, after a period spent in the wilderness, Hollywood had made a resounding comeback. This was followed by other artistic developments, such as the acquisition of major paintings and sculptures by American galleries and museums.

Science followed art, and there was footage of a couple of American physicists being awarded the Nobel Prize for their work in unifying quantum mechanics and astrophysics. Attention was also devoted to pharmaceutical breakthroughs in relation to Parkinson's, multiple sclerosis and several orphan diseases. Good work had been done on the ageing gene and medical intervention to prolong life would not be far behind. The implication was that Silicon Valley had increased its lead over other countries in terms of technological innovation.

By mid-year the space programme had identified a second enormous solar system two hundred lightyears from Earth, and additional black holes. There was growing evidence of life on Titan.

American oil companies had made major

progress in developing systems of leak-proof carbon capture; these systems were expected to halt global warming in its tracks without any need to economise on carbon emissions. The narrator's *basso profundo* seemed to lend an authenticity to the unfolding, upbeat tapestry.

"This is certainly the Hollywood feel-good version," Tim said, laughing.

"Propaganda," Patrick grated. He was far from amused. There was no mention of America's continuing military interventions in the Middle East, of the abandonment of the Developing World, of its refusal to sign up to eco-friendly protocols, or of the fact that America's military spending was now almost two-thirds of world spending. If these realities were deliberately omitted, what hope was there? His annoyance grew as he saw Dwyer sharing a joke with Evelyn Ralston.

When the applause died down Bob introduced the next segment, the time capsule. Celebrities brought items on stage which were described by Bob and then placed in the capsule. The items ranged from newly revealed samples of moon rock to the latest computer chips, from modern wonder drugs to revolutionary prosthetic devices and artificial hearts, from organically grown foods to genetically modified substitutes, from works of literature and art (copies) to music scores, from architectural *maquettes* to small devices manufactured by nanotechnology. As a gesture to popular culture, a version of the most recently designed hamburger carton was placed near the top of the time capsule.

No weapons of any sort, Patrick noted, oblivious of surrounding laughter, only those things and services that added to human welfare. The US had a limitless appetite for these fruits and that was what would drive the country for the generation to come. All gain and no pain. That meant others doing the work. And that meant some form of re-colonisation, not excluding China, which had already become the workshop of America.

He sat upright to see Evelyn leave the table after a whispered conference with Dwyer. He watched her weave through the hall, heading for the exit. Then he saw Dwyer furtively leave the table and move in the same direction. A tryst. It had to be. His heartbeat quickened as he glanced at his watch. Ten thirty. It was possible that Dwyer would not return. The moment had come; he had to act now. Grim-faced, he got to his feet and muttered some excuse. He walked quickly between the tables hoping he hadn't left it too late. For a moment he lost sight of Dwyer and thought that he had already left the room. But then he saw him again near one of the bars, where he had run into a group of acquaintances. Patrick took the spectacles from his pocket and approached the bar. He ordered a drink and inched towards Dwyer, who was still in conversation with a small group of people. He held the spectacles in his right hand.

"…a pity Amanda couldn't come," one of the men was saying. "Give her our regards."

"Yes, I will," Dwyer said, looking at his watch. "There's someone else I have to see. If you'll excuse me…"

Holding the drink in his left hand, Patrick stepped back from the bar and stumbled against Dwyer.

"Watch it!"

"Sorry." He brought his right hand up and made contact with Dwyer's wrist.

"Are you drunk?"

"Sorry. My fault" Patrick ambled away. Before he got back to the table he looked behind him and saw that Dwyer had gone out of the hall. This was a stroke of luck. The poison would take about fifteen minutes to act. So, it might happen outside the room. For the first time in over a month Patrick allowed himself to think more positively about his own chances of survival.

He went to a restroom and locked himself into one of the stalls. He examined the small syringe; it was half-empty. That was more than enough. He made a wad of toilet paper, injected the rest of the fluid into it and flushed it away. Then he carefully broke the spectacles, wrapped each piece in toilet paper and flushed them away one by one.

Outside, he washed and dried his hands. He saw his face in the mirror and was mildly surprised that it hadn't changed. He splashed water into his eyes and dried himself on a roller towel.

When he got back to the table he sensed that Maura knew. Her face was a mask but she couldn't say anything in the presence of the others. The O'Malleys were arguing with the Germans about what kind of hamburger carton had gone into the time capsule.

"No, it was definitely a McDonald's," the German insisted.

"You must be blind," Tim said. "It's a Burger King. The Home of the Whopper."

"We don't have them in Germany."

"Just because you don't have them in Germany doesn't mean they don't exist."

"That is very Hegelian." The man roared with laughter and raised his glass to nobody in particular.

"No, it's just common sense," Tim replied, bending forward to allow Clare to straighten his bow tie.

"Ah, you are an empiricist," the German said, looking around to see if he had acquired an audience.

"I know what I saw."

"But can we rely on sense perception?" The German threw out his large hands in an effort to embrace this concept. "We sometimes see what we want to see. Is that not so?"

"Well, I don't know about you," Tim said, "But I see what's there. I deal in facts, hard facts."

"Pack it in," Clare whispered to him. "He's just a bullshit artist," she added by way of explanation.

Tim smiled crookedly at her. "Bullshit artistry, my dear, is the safety valve of civilisation." He returned to the fray, to the delight of the German party.

Evelyn's aide was taken unawares by her sudden departure and he rushed out after her. Through his earpiece he heard a colleague say that she had walked on her own through the lobby and entered the elevator, probably on her way up to the fourth floor suite.

"Why would she do that?" He spoke into his cuff.

"I don't know, man. But you better get up there fast."

He pushed his way through the crowds and rode up in the elevator. He knocked at the door of the suite.

"Be with you in a minute." Evelyn's voice sang out. When she opened the door she looked at him in surprise. "What are you doing here?"

"It's my job, Ma'am."

"I don't want you following me around."

"But I have to … I'll just stay here in the corridor."

"No, you won't. I'm not a goddam prisoner on parole. I want you to leave. Now."

"I've got my orders…"

"Well, I'm countermanding them. Go. Just go away. Downstairs. Now." She made a shooing gesture with her hands.

He hesitated, but she faced him down until he left. Partly to cover his own flanks, he immediately sought out Corcoran and reported what had happened. Evelyn put a bottle of Finnish vodka on ice and opened a jar of Beluga. Then she went into the bathroom, refreshed her make-up and dabbed a little perfume behind her ears. She wondered what was keeping Lawrence.

CHAPTER 19

PATRICK NEEDED A drink; he couldn't remember where he'd put the one he'd used as a prop when he approached Dwyer. The sense of relief hadn't lasted long. He felt depressed and could only imagine what Maura was feeling. He reached for her hand as if some physical contact would help them, but she moved away from him.

The conversation with the Germans died away as the orchestra struck up. Tim asked Maura to dance and Clare turned to Patrick.

"Let's see what you're made of."

With an effort of will he got to his feet. Clare kept the conversation going as they danced.

"Some people got nostalgic on these occasions," she remarked. "Even a little down."

"I'm afraid I fall in that camp." He was grateful for the excuse she supplied him with. They managed to avoid an elderly couple who were doing some ancient variant of the jitterbug.

"You know, I think Tim is too," Clare said. "Only he masks it with booze and tries to rise to the occasion."

"I'm not very good company, I'm afraid," Patrick said.

"Nonsense," Clare responded. "You're a

nice man. We can't all be extroverts." Out of the corner of her eye she saw an elderly man trying to do the Lambada with a Hollywood queen. She drew Patrick's attention to the scene, hoping it might cheer him up.

The tempo of the music quickened and Clare decided not to put Patrick through any more.

"This is a bit fast for me," she said. They walked back to the table.

Corcoran had followed Dwyer out of the Lincoln Room and kept tabs on him until he went into Evelyn's suite. With almost twenty-five years' experience under his belt, Corcoran was unfazed by this turn of events, though he was intrigued by it. As he walked away he was satisfied that whatever was about to happen behind that door, security concerns were not at issue.

"This is crazy, Lawrence." Evelyn locked the door behind him.

"I know," he said, "but that never stopped us before, did it?"

"We were younger then." She offered him a drink. She was suddenly nervous like a homecoming queen, overawed by the brass bands, flags and banners.

"No thanks." He took her in his arms. They were young lovers again, hungry for each other. Between kisses her eyes wandered over his face as if she needed to be assured that this was really happening. Gradually she relaxed; her gown slipped to the floor. Her skin melted at his touch.

Their love-making had the benefit of remembered pleasure and the urgency of making up for lost time. She climaxed shortly after he entered her and that triggered his orgasm. But she knew, of old, how to revive him. He had once told her how an uncircumcised man liked to be touched; she hadn't forgotten. This time they rode a wilder tide that rose and rose to a pitch of almost unbearable intensity that carried them inexorably towards release. They lay gasping.

"Oh, Lawrence … How I needed you all those years."

"We needed each other … I've waited a long time."

"So have I. Christ, I was so weak. I should have run away with you that time in my parents' house…" She stroked his face.

"And disobeyed your father?"

"He was such a bastard. I never forgave him. Do you forgive me?" She gazed into his eyes and laid her cheek against his. He kissed the downy hair at her temples.

"Of course. You were young. It was an emotional conflict. But I never fully understood why you married Stanley." The sounds of the orchestra drifted faintly into the room; some up-tempo number that seemed at odds with their mood.

"If I couldn't have you it really made little

difference who I married." She turned her head and light caught the gleam of sweat in the salt cellar of her throat.

He mulled this over for a while and she asked him what he was thinking.

"I suppose it was much the same with Amanda and me. We went our own ways from day one. Still do."

"Are you happy with that, Lawrence?"

"I don't honestly know what happiness is. I'm content. I have my work…"

"Ah, work." She laughed. "Some things don't change."

"No." He laughed too. "I guess I'm better with machines than people. They're more predictable. You make them and they do what they're supposed to do. If they don't you redesign them until they do."

"You're a control freak. Is that why you dabble in politics?"

"Politicians are a little like machines. You know what they want. Each one has an instruction manual. If you can read that and push the right buttons then you get the desired result. It's pretty straightforward. They come in slightly different models but the basic engineering is the same." Following a faint knock a chambermaid, using a pass key, stuck her head around the door and inquired nervously if they wanted the bed turned down.

"No," Evelyn said sharply. "Out." She pointed to the door. "Imagine," she said to

Lawrence, "no one told her this was a specially allocated room. I'll have to mention it to the management. It really isn't good enough."

He looked at her in surprise, smiling faintly. She calmed down quickly and asked him to go on.

"There's not much more to say."

"But why do you have so much … business … with Stanley?" She was keen to know if his desire to influence her husband had something to do with reducing him in her eyes.

"Because he's there," Lawrence said lightly.

"Is that the only reason?"

"What other reason might there be? We have interests in common."

"I just wondered…" She let it pass for the moment.

They lay back. The night was peaceful; all was well. They were celebrating the turn of the century in their own way and with clear consciences; infidelity was a mere technicality.

"So where do we go from here?" Evelyn asked at length.

"A good question."

"Well, I'm certainly not going to march you up the aisle." She laughed.

"And divorce the CASA man? I should hope not."

"We really should try to see each other more often though," Evelyn said in a definite tone.

"Absolutely. That's got my vote." Sounds of

roistering drifted in from outside – young people spilling on to the streets, preparing to celebrate in their own way. At least there would be public displays; fireworks at the Tidal Basin, military bands on the Mall, pop groups in Rock-Creek Park.

"We would have to be very careful though." Evelyn quite liked the idea of intrigue, secret trysts, mysterious visits to the West Coast.

"Yes. We can't afford to embarrass Stanley." Lawrence was not being sarcastic; he too had a vested interest in Stanley's re-election. He looked at his watch. "God, the countdown."

"Skip it." She fondled him.

"Duty calls. I promised to do it."

"What about your duty to me?"

"That's not a duty. That's something else."

They got out of bed and helped and hindered each other dressing. There was something at the back of her mind – yes, that political stuff Lillian had been feeding her. Well, it could wait. Starting an affair was going to be wonderful, slipping out of the house when Stanley was away, meeting in secret locations, not excluding Europe and Latin America. She would have to be extremely careful though, especially where William was concerned. He would like nothing better than to catch her out in an indiscretion and use it against her. Still, she could handle him. Yes, her life was taking an exciting turn and it wasn't a rehearsal. She would make the most of it.

She noticed Lawrence struggling with his cuff- links and went to his assistance. She drew his attention to the slightly yellow stain on his left cuff.

"What's that?"

"Probably a body fluid." He grinned. "Or maybe it was that drunk who collided with me at the bar. What is it, eggnog?" He sniffed it, spat on the corner of a silk handkerchief and rubbed it vigorously.

"Well, keep it hidden," she advised. "We want our very special host looking his best."

He left first, and after a discreet interval she followed.

Shortly after she returned to the Lincoln Room she heard a familiar voice behind her and turned to see a Giaconda smile on Lillian's face.

"My, my, two people conspicuous by their absence. What does it all mean?"

" God, it's like running the gauntlet," Evelyn protested. First the security man, then the chambermaid, now my best friend.

Lillian put a hand under her elbow and led her to a quiet alcove. "Well, well, spit it out."

Evelyn considered a smart retort but in the event said, "It was wonderful. It was so good to see him again after all those years."

"Did you get a chance to talk to him?" Lillian cut to the chase.

"About what?"

"Oh, Christ."

"Give me a break," Evelyn said. "I'm not going to start lecturing the man on day one. Besides, have you ever heard of subtlety?"

"Hmmm." Lillian wondered if she would ever get round to it. She knew that Evelyn had a lot of virtues but the common weal did not loom large among them. She let it go for now and changed tack, "So you're walking on air."

"You could say that." It was Evelyn's turn to smile mysteriously. "Yes, I believe you could say that."

"I'm sure I could. You're going to have to decide, you know."

"On what?"

"Isn't it obvious?"

"No. What are you driving at?"

Lillian bent closer. "Are you going to leave Stanley?"

"Slow down for god's sake." Evelyn gave a short laugh that was almost like a snort.

"You can't have everything." Lillian displayed just a trace of irritation.

"Why not?" Evelyn seemed genuinely puzzled and wondered if her long-time friend was not a little jealous. Her question remained unanswered.

Patrick tensed up when he saw Bob go to the

centre of the stage to make an announcement, but he was shaken to the core when he saw Dwyer follow him out to the microphone.

What had gone wrong? The syringe must not have broken the skin. The fluid must have gone into the material of his clothing. He would have to act again, and this time in plain sight. There were no options left. His heart raced as Bob began a little speech welcoming the New Year and introducing his boss, Lawrence T. Dwyer. There was mention of several sponsoring companies, especially KNYBS, but none of Kaltronics.

Dwyer made a few comments, welcoming everyone to the party and wishing one and all a healthy and prosperous new year. After a minute or so of these lazy clichés he consulted his watch and began the countdown, "Ten, nine, eight …" The crowd joined in noisily.

For Patrick it was literally a matter of seconds. Fighting off a dizzy spell, he reached back with his right hand and released the safety catch. He stood and walked slowly towards the stage, the gun still hidden. But he was now in plain sight.

"Where's he going?" Clare asked.

"Damned if I know," Tim replied. "Maybe he's going to say a few words on behalf of the prize-winners."

"That would be nice," Clare said. "A few words of thanks from us to the sponsors. I hope that's it. If not, you should do it."

"Why me? You always say the patriarchy gets all the good jobs. You're a strong woman. Empower yourself. You do it."

"Maybe I will." She opened her purse, fished out a small diary pen and started writing some notes on a napkin.

Satisfied with the success of his ploy, Tim took a large sip of his single malt whiskey – Jameson Reserve.

Maura was frozen into immobility. She tried to stand, perhaps to follow Patrick, impede him in some way, but her legs would not support her.

"…four … three … two…"

Thinking of his brother, Jean, Patrick drew the pistol. For some reason Dwyer looked up at that moment and saw this figure standing before him, gun in hand. He strained to recognise, then flinched.

"No!" Maura cried out. "No!"

From the balcony, Corcoran shouted and reached for his revolver.

A shot rang out. Dwyer slumped. Patrick fired again. Then one of the security men leapt forward and shot him through the head.

There was pandemonium in the hall. Guests screamed and sprang away from where the two bodies lay. Bells rang out and thousands of balloons and streamers floated down from the ceiling. 'Auld Lang Syne' blared out from the sound system and was suddenly stopped.

Security men pushed through the crowd.

Corcoran jumped from the mezzanine onto the stage. He used the microphone to call for a doctor and ambulance, and shouted for the doors to be locked. No one was to leave the hall. Another man bent over Dwyer, searching for a pulse and shook his head. At the back of the hall a number of men moved towards the doors and formed a cordon.

Long before the paramedics arrived the hotel doctor pronounced both men dead.

Maura tried to get through the crowd to Patrick but her way was blocked. She could see his hand hanging limply from the table on which his body sprawled. She remembered his advice to walk away but she couldn't do it. A dazed Tim O'Malley forced a way through for her. She wanted to cradle Patrick's head but the security men wouldn't let her touch the body. Corcoran told her to make herself available for questioning later, and nodded to one of his men to keep her under surveillance.

The O'Malleys and the other prize-winners looked aghast at her, not knowing what to say but sensing that she was implicated in some way. When the hysteria died down it was possible to hear the sounds of revelry outside the hotel, fireworks exploding in the sky, sirens, fog horns, church bells.

Evelyn sat trembling. Lillian stayed close to her and advised her not to show any emotion. When her aide suggested that she should leave she agreed immediately. They had no difficulty getting her through the cordon. Lillian stayed behind to cover the story to the bitter end. She had a journalist's instinct that the assassin might have shared her theory about the future course of America, though that was no justification for what he had done.

Bob Carraway had been at the side of the stage when the gunman approached. Everything seemed to stop for a few seconds before the first shot was fired. He thought he'd been hit and actually checked himself for signs of blood. Only when he saw Dwyer fall did he realise he was safe, but he was in shock; his stomach heaved. He could hardly believe that his boss was dead.

The police arrived in force and prevented the paramedics from removing the bodies until they had completed their examinations and taken several photographs. While this was going on Lillian approached Maura and tried to interview her. She wanted to establish her relationship to the assassin and the reasons for targeting Lawrence Dwyer. Tim advised Maura not to say anything; the advice was unnecessary. Lillian persisted until Corcoran intervened and ordered her away. He told Maura to stay where she was.

While the police questioned other witnesses, the O'Malleys stayed close to Maura as if giving her moral support. They remained silent, however, bewildered by what had happened and not knowing the extent of

Maura's involvement. A little later they were questioned by a patrolman who logged their evidence.

Eventually the bodies were removed and Maura was led away by Corcoran and two other agents. The O'Malleys' sad, perplexed gaze followed her to the door. She was placed in an unmarked car and driven in silence to the nearest police station. There she was led to a small interview room and left on her own for a while. She felt the walls closing in on her and couldn't catch her breath. Her vision became clouded and she tried to focus on the grain of the wooden table. Her eyes went back in her head and she passed out.

When she came to, a police doctor was standing over her. He helped her to drink some water and offered her a sedative which she refused. Corcoran nodded to him and he left the room.

"We need to ask you some questions." Corcoran didn't give a damn about Lawrence Dwyer but he knew how well connected he was. What irritated him most was that he, himself, had failed, and that one failure would destroy his hitherto spotless record. The Bureau was unforgiving, especially when incidents like this got into the press, which it undoubtedly would. Equally galling was the fact that earlier in the evening he had actually observed the assassin behaving in an odd way. OK, he was one of a list of about twenty that Corcoran had

had some doubts about. But still … One thing was certain: he would never mention that particular event to his Bureau chiefs. He was in enough trouble as it was.

There were two other people present in the interview room, including a uniformed female officer. Corcoran switched on a tape-recorder and they listened intently as the story came out piece by piece. Maura broke down several times and they had to wait until she recovered. When they had a broad outline Corcoran summarised, "You're saying that the assassin was posing as your husband, that your real husband was kidnapped in England and this man took his place? Have I got it right so far?"

Maura nodded.

"Please." He gestured towards the recording machine.

"Yes."

"And what was this man's name?"

"Patrick," she said.

"Second name?"

She had to think hard. Had she ever heard it? No, she loved him but didn't even know his name. It was as if he'd never existed. A sense of despair surged through her, a sadness that was beyond tears.

"I … don't know it."

"He obviously wasn't acting on his own," Corcoran said. "What group did he represent?"

"Some revolutionary movement…"

"Based in France?" His eyes never left her

face.

"I … think so." Her mouth was dry. She sipped the water the doctor had left. Patrick was dead; that fact overwhelmed her.

"Any link to ISIS or Arab terrorism?"

"I … I don't think so …

"And what was the motivation?"

"Peace…"

"Peace? Kind of ironic, don't you think?"

"He … they believe that arms manufacturers help to cause wars…"

"I see." Corcoran told one of the officers to check with the International Crime Unit and the CIA. Then he turned his attention back to Maura. "Can the British Police verify that your husband was kidnapped?"

"They … don't know."

Corcoran pursed his lips; it was clear that this didn't sit right with him. He gave her the impression that she was on very thin ice. He wrote something in a notepad and, from beneath a pile of papers, he produced Harold's passport which he passed across the table to her.

"This is your husband's passport?"

"Yes."

"And despite the likeness you say that the man we have in the morgue is not your husband?"

"That's correct. He … he put grey dye in his hair and…"

"We can check on that," Corcoran said.

"The clothes we took off the body were English made."

"He must have been in England for some time before my … husband was kidnapped." She began to feel faint again and gripped the edge of the table not just for support but for some sense of reality. The thought of Patrick lying on a slab somewhere was too much to bear. The officer returned with a cup of tea which he wordlessly placed beside her.

"You had been with this man, Patrick, for over a week in New York and for some days here in Washington. You knew what he was planning to do."

"Not exactly … He didn't want me to be involved…"

"That was very thoughtful of him. But you suspected?"

"Yes."

"So you were an accessory."

"They threatened to kill my husband. What could I do?" She was being disingenuous and knew it. At the beginning it was true but after her affair with Patrick began and when she knew that Harold would be freed whatever the outcome, her concern had switched to Patrick. She couldn't deny that to herself but she couldn't admit it to this man. What if they established that she had been sleeping with Patrick? The O'Malleys must have known. Now that she was heading into deep waters her senses became more alert.

"Couldn't you have warned Mr. Dwyer?" Corcoran examined the tips of his fingers and then looked closely at her.

"Then the security men would have acted and…" She stopped abruptly. She was going to say that Patrick would have resisted and been killed.

"And what?" Corcoran pressed.

"The people holding my husband would have killed him…"

"How would they know that it was you who blew the whistle?"

Her blood ran cold and she fought hard to maintain some sort of composure. She tasted the tea mainly to buy time. "They wouldn't have to know that … The fact that they failed would be enough…"

"You think they would have killed your husband just because their mission failed?"

"Yes."

"But you don't know them. How could you have been so sure of that?" He wrote something else on the note pad.

"Look," she said, "I wasn't sure of anything. But I couldn't afford to take the risk. What was I supposed to do? Tell me … tell me…"

He didn't say anything else, but gestured to the others and they left the room. The woman officer stayed behind. It was almost three a.m. and Maura's nervous energy began to drain away, leaving her exhausted. She heard hysterical, incoherent shouting coming from another room and looked up in alarm.

"Heroin, most like," the woman officer said in an off-hand way. "Don't worry about it."

When Corcoran returned he stood in the middle of the room staring down at her. "We're not going to arrest you. Not yet at least. But a female officer will accompany you to the hotel and stay with you until we make contact again."

Maura was too exhausted to object. Besides, she thought it was better to co-operate in every way possible. Before she left, Corcoran asked her if there was anything she wanted to say to them. There was something about his expression that suggested it was a loaded question.

"I presume," she said, "that you will be in touch with the British police."

"Of course."

It was probably her imagination but she thought a flicker of disappointment passed over his features.

Maura crept into bed just as the dawn was coming up. The woman officer – the one who had been in the interview room – settled herself in front of the TV. She was on the graveyard shift. They had spoken little on the way to the hotel.

Maura was too tired to sleep. She thought of going to the kitchen to make tea but couldn't bring herself to do it. The memory of sitting in the kitchen with Patrick was too fresh in her mind. She wept silently.

The next day the assassination was in all the papers and news bulletins. Some of the guests who had witnessed it were media people and the coverage was detailed and accurate. There was even a photograph of Lawrence falling after being shot; one of the guests must have sold a copy from a phone. There was considerable speculation about motive and a couple of journalists came close to the truth. One actually suggested that the Active Peace Force may have been behind it. One cynical columnist said it was appropriate that a violent year should have ended the way it did.

CHAPTER 20

ALLOWING FOR THE time difference, Paul did not call Paris until 7 a.m. GMT on the first of January. He dialled directly from a kiosk in Saffron Walden, gave his mobile number to the contact in Paris and waited to be called back. It was bitterly cold and the fields and roads were covered in hoar frost. He had an intimation that the operation had not gone well. On hearing the dial tone, he brought the phone to his ear.

"Well?"

"Both," the voice said.

"Our man too?"

"Yes."

"Christ."

"Get out now."

"OK." Paul hung up and leant against the wall. He had always known that Patrick would take whatever risk was necessary but he had hoped it would not come to this.

He got into the car and drove back to the old farm-house, taking care to slow down when he came upon patches of black ice. In a couple of hours the news would cross the Atlantic and the police would start a manhunt. The plan was to lie low in London for a couple of weeks and then to make their way to Rome. But first they would drive north to Cambridge, abandon the car and take the train to Liverpool Street

Station.

He helped his comrade clear their stuff out of the farmhouse and made sure that nothing incriminating was left behind. He was going to put on the balaclava and tell Harold he was free to go, but he decided against it. Instead, he silently drew back the bolt on the cellar door. Let the fool figure it out for himself, he thought. He took one last look around the derelict room that had been their home for the past two weeks. Then he got into the Toyota beside the driver and spread the map across his knees. A little over an hour later they had reached the outskirts of Cambridge. They drove down Trumpington Street and turned right at the war monument for Station Road.

Harold was up and about. He wondered why they hadn't brought him anything to eat and why the shorter man hadn't come to let him slop out. It was quieter than usual upstairs and he thought he'd heard the car engine earlier that morning. But it didn't occur to him to try the door. He was aware it was New Year's Day although that meant little to him. What were those bastards up to, he thought angrily, and when in god's name were they going to release him? He dragged the cot over to where a shaft of light from the window allowed him read. He lay down and opened the yellowing paperback, a thriller by an unheard-of author. He had been eking it out for the last few days, trying his best to make the characters come alive. It was dreadful stuff but it was all he had. No doubt it was the sort of rubbish those idiots in the balaclavas would relish.

He finished the chapter and decided to save the next one for later in the day. Although the battery in the old transistor radio was giving up the ghost he switched on the set in the hope of getting some financial news. He surfed the channels, heard snatches of techno music and rap and the inane ape chatter of DJs. He was about to switch off the set to conserve the battery when he caught a newsflash that made him sit bolt upright. Lawrence Dwyer had been assassinated at a function in Washington DC. His killer had also been shot dead. An English woman was helping police with their inquiries. Maura! It had to be Maura. She'd really done it this time.

Only then did it occur to him that his captors might have left. He went to pound on the door which opened after the first blow of his fist. With as little noise as possible he went diffidently up the rotting staircase. When he got to the top he slowly pushed open the door that led to the ground floor and peered through cautiously. If they were still there they might punish him for trying to escape, but he couldn't see any sign of them.

As he grew in confidence, he went further into the room which he knew they had occupied. It looked as if it had been recently swept out and there were no provisions or sleeping bags. An oil stain on a wooden crate showed where they had probably done their primitive cooking with some kind of camping stove. They had gone all right, the bastards, without telling him. There was no sign of the car outside, though he discerned what he thought were fresh tyre tracks.

He was free. He filled his lungs with the cold, fresh air and started to cough. For a while he was confused, not knowing what to do. He went back to the cellar as if there might be something there which he wanted to bring with him. But anything of any value was in the pockets of the jacket he was wearing – and had been wearing virtually around the clock. His beard was almost fully grown and he knew that he smelled. It occurred to him that the police would probably examine the cellar in detail so he left it as it was, with one exception. He slopped- out for the last time and flung the bucket as far as he could into an overgrown field behind the house where it fell into a patch of briars and wild nettles. That had been the symbol of his greatest ignominy and he didn't want anyone else to know about it.

He trudged down the muddy lane, following the tyre tracks. When he reached the road his shoes were in a sorry state and his feet were cold and wet. He hoped against hope that he might come across his car. He fantasised about driving home, sneaking into the house unnoticed, having a warm bath, a brandy or two, then going to the police and tackling them about their ineptitude. It was not to be.

Two cars passed him during the first half hour and neither stopped. He cursed the drivers under his breath; they had obviously assumed that he was a vagrant of some kind. He continued to walk, partly to keep warm. He knew that he was going in a southerly direction but since he didn't know his starting point he had no idea where he was headed for. He hadn't come across any road signs and the terrain looked unfamiliar.

He tried to remember how long the journey had been from the golf club; his best guess was anywhere between one and three hours and that didn't help at all. The only thing he could be sure of was that it was a farming area; many of the fields were ploughed and some were waterlogged. Maybe it wasn't too far away from Fen country but that was cold comfort since few people came there in winter.

His anxiety grew. It wasn't long since the winter solstice and it would grow dark at about four o'clock. If he had to spend the night in a ditch he would probably freeze to death. At least there were a couple of blankets in the cellar. But the thought of using his new-found freedom to go back to that awful place was abhorrent to him. He decided to walk to the next turn in the road. If there were no houses or road signs in view he would have to reconsider. Praying under his breath he walked as fast as he could. A flock of crows broke from a leafless copse of trees and startled him. They descended on a ploughed field searching for worms in the heavy brown earth.

From the next bend the road stretched away into the distance. There was no sign of life and a chilling mist began to descend. Panic seized him. He turned around and walked back the way he had come. The cellar now seemed a welcoming prospect. It offered the reassurance of familiarity. As well as the blankets, he had candles, a book and a radio – and it was only an hour away.

He had walked about a mile when he saw in the distance an oddly shaped vehicle coming towards him. He narrowed his eyes and made it out to be a tractor pulling a trailer. He moved to the crown of the narrow road and started to wave his arms. The farmer had no option but to stop.

"Could you give me a lift please?" Harold cried out, ashamed of the beseeching note in his voice.

"Well, I dunno." The farmer looked him up and down. "Where're you headed?"

"The next town," Harold said. He didn't want to admit that he had no idea what the next town was.

"I'm goin' to Saffron Walden."

"That's it," Harold said excitedly. "Saffron Walden. Me too." He was just about to offer payment when the farmer told him to hop up on the trailer. He said something else about 'good pickin's this time of year', but Harold didn't catch it all. He sat on the cleanest part of the trailer he could find. The smell was atrocious and to his horror he felt dampness seep through his trousers. The farmer put the tractor into gear and they lurched off. The bumping of the trailer on the rutted road seemed to release new and more virulent odours. At first Harold thought that the organic matter that littered the flat bed of the trailer was a sort of silage but on closer inspection he realised it was the residue of pig slops. That's what the farmer meant by good pickings. After the over-indulgence of New Year's Eve there would be an abundance of slops for the pigs. Harold was already sitting in the Christmas left-overs. He felt humiliated; this was the final indignity. He resolved to get those French shits if it was the last thing he ever did. At one point the left wheel of the trailer hit a pot-hole in the road and pitched him sideways into a deeper layer of rotting matter. Nothing would compensate for this. The only thing that helped him survive this awful journey was the feeling of anger that built up in him and the desire for revenge.

When he was eventually dropped in the town he waited for a moment until the farmer drove away. He managed to locate a comb in his inside pocket and he used it to scrape off as much of the loose matter from his clothes as he could. A few passers-by stared hard at him but gave him a very wide berth. As he knew the layout of the town reasonably well, he managed to locate the police station and presented himself to the duty sergeant who was distinctly unimpressed by the story he heard.

"I tell you I was kidnapped," Harold repeated.

"Tell the Sally Army," the sergeant said patiently "Go on, off with you. We can't do anything for you here."

Harold slammed his wallet down on the counter. "Look, I've got ID. I'm a dentist."

The sergeant looked briefly at the contents of the wallet. "Because of the day that's in it, I'm going to turn a blind eye to this…"

"What?"

"Go on now before I nick you for lifting some bloke's wallet. Hop it."

Harold felt faint. There was no end to the nightmare. Had he not endured enough already? If he could only hire a taxi or minicab but no one would take him in the condition he was in. He probably had enough cash for a cheap suit if he could find a shop open. Yes, that was probably the best bet in the circumstances. He stretched out his hand to retrieve the wallet.

"Oh no you don't, mate," the sergeant said. "This is the property of Mr. Harold Crowther."

"I'm Harold Crowther…"

"Go on now. Get out of here before I change my mind."

Harold gritted his teeth and added the

sergeant to his revenge list, but if he failed to control his temper now all would be lost. He also sensed that if he mentioned the assassination in Washington the sergeant would consider him mad.

"Look, sergeant," he said in his best accent," "I know I look like a tramp and it would take a long time to explain how that came about. But please listen to me…" He went on to say that he knew the number of every credit card in the wallet and invited the sergeant to put him to the test. The sergeant said he was not in the mood for playing games but he seemed a little less judgmental than before, and reluctantly allowed Harold to make a phone call.

Harold wasn't sure who he should call. There would be no one at the surgery and his golf partners might be out. He decided that Barbara Woodside was the best bet. She would be curious enough to come and pick him up.

When he finally got through he tried to explain the situation to her as best he could despite her repeated interruptions.

"I knew it," she said. "I knew it all along…"

"Could you come over now, Barbara."

"I'm on my way," she said excitedly.

Approximately an hour later she came bustling through the doors of the police station. "I knew it. I just knew it…"

She was about to embrace him when she

noticed the state he was in. He drew her aside.

"Don't say anything to the local plod. Just vouch for me. I'll explain later."

Barbara was as good as her word and the sergeant handed over the wallet. He still wasn't particularly interested in unearthing whatever story lay behind this odd situation. Stranger things happened at sea.

Barbara fetched a rug from the boot of her car and spread it on the passenger seat for Harold to sit on. On the drive to Hertingfordbury she plagued him with questions. Although he didn't give very full answers she managed to piece most of it together and her eyes grew rounder and wider.

"My god, it goes right to the top," she said a number of times. "This is so big. I heard it on the news this morning. Of course I didn't make the connection then. But now…"

She told him about her call to the hotel in Washington, and about the man who answered. "A Jacques Montret," she recalled without any difficulty. "He said he knew you."

"He must've been the assassin." Harold wondered where Maura was when all this was taking place.

"Christ. Of course. And I was talking to him just an hour or two before … it happened." Her cheeks became flushed and her driving rather erratic. Her pupils were never going to believe this.

When she dropped him at his home she

said, "Listen, as soon as you've tidied yourself up we'll go straight to Scotland Yard."

"No," he said firmly. "I'm grateful for your help but this is something I must handle myself." The thought of her poking her nose in at this late stage left him cold.

"But I…"

"No, Barbara. I don't want to involve you. There's more to this than meets the eye," he added cryptically.

Although the house looked entirely familiar he felt as if he were an intruder who had broken into some rich man's home. He tore off his filthy clothes and threw them in a bin outside the back door. While the bath was running he gave his teeth the first proper brushing they'd had in weeks. His gums bled from accumulated plaque until he used a special mouthwash to staunch the blood. To save time he only trimmed the beard.

He went downstairs and defrosted a loaf of bread and some cold cuts and made himself a triple-decker sandwich. He poured himself a large brandy and brought it and the sandwich back upstairs to the bathroom where he lowered himself with grunts of pleasure into the hot, soapy water.

When he'd finished his meal and ablutions he dressed in his best suit and went downstairs. He got the telephone directory out of a drawer and looked up the number for Scotland Yard.

Later that day the female officer told Maura that she had to present herself for another interview. A patrol car was sent for them and as they left the hotel Maura saw a number of guests, including the O'Malleys, board a coach for the airport. The holiday of a lifetime was well and truly over. She didn't know that the O'Malleys had tried to make contact with her but were prevented from doing so. She hoped to have an opportunity of meeting them again.

They went to the same precinct as before but the interview was conducted in a different, slightly larger room. Maura immediately asked about Harold and was told that he was free and unharmed.

"But there are still some questions we would like to put to you," Corcoran said. "Do you happen to know where ... em ... Patrick obtained the firearm?"

"No. I think he may have bought it in Washington but I can't be sure." It was probably the day he returned with flowers and presented them to her in the bath.

"He didn't bring it from London?"

"I don't think so."

"And the poison?" Corcoran sat on a corner of the table looking down at her.

"What?"

"We found traces of a lethal substance in

the cuff of Mr. Dwyer's shirt. It would have been enough to kill him had it penetrated the skin."

"I don't know anything about that." She realized that Patrick must have tried that before the shooting. If it had worked he would probably be alive now. Why hadn't he just cut his losses?

"He would have brought that with him from London. Did you notice a phial or small glass container in his luggage?"

"No."

"Or something that might have contained a small syringe. A pen for example?"

"I don't think so." She realised now how right Patrick had been not to tell her about the details.

"You travelled together. You stayed in the same hotel, in the same suite. You must have seen his luggage."

"He had a suit bag, an old one, and a briefcase but he kept them to himself."

Corcoran then gestured to an officer who laid a spectacle case on the table. Corcoran removed the glasses. "Have you seen these before?"

"Yes. He wore those glasses to make him look like my husband."

"But they don't quite fit the case." Corcoran demonstrated this to her. "Did he have a second pair, perhaps with steel frames?"

"I don't think so. Only those horn-rimmed

ones." She had no idea what Corcoran was driving at and she had no intention of asking. She had a feeling that her big trial was yet to begin.

He then asked her to give a chronological account of the night in question. He concentrated mainly on the times that Patrick had left the table and where she thought he had gone. She answered truthfully and had the impression that she was merely confirming what other witnesses, including the O'Malleys, had said. Then he changed tack.

"Did he ever mention why he wanted to kill Mr. Dwyer?"

"Not as such," Maura said carefully. She didn't want to give the impression that Patrick had confided in her. Of course he hadn't, but because of their closeness she was able to infer quite a lot. "I think it had something to do with armaments."

"Anything else?"

"Possibly the fact that Mr. Dwyer had a lot of influence with the Government. He didn't say that. It's really surmise on my part."

"Did he mention anything about his own organisation?"

She was conscious that Corcoran was going over old ground. She tried to be consistent with what she'd said before. "Not that I can remember."

"Does Active Peace Force or APF mean anything to you?" His expression never changed; she had no idea what was going through his head.

"I think I've heard of it ... some radical group. But he didn't mention it."

"OK, Mrs. Crowther, one last question. Did you sleep with him?" He asked this without any modulation in his tone.

"No!" Her face flushed scarlet from embarrassment but it could have passed for indignation. Either way it did not inhibit Corcoran.

"You shared a suite together..."

"Two rooms," she interrupted without meaning to.

"You're an attractive woman, Mrs. Crowther. Are you saying he never made a pass."

"That is exactly what I'm saying. And even if he had, nothing would have happened. I'm a married woman. He was responsible for kidnapping my husband, for god's sake..." She locked her fingers together to stop her hands from trembling. From the corner of her eye she could see the golden gleam of her wedding band.

"And you have a good relationship with your husband?"

"Of course. We've been happily married for fifteen years." She was about to object to this line of questioning when he excused himself and left the room.

Maura tried her best to appear composed.

She was almost certain that he'd gone out to confer with someone else who had probably been watching the proceedings through a one-way mirror. She caught the eye of the woman officer who gave her what seemed to be a sympathetic nod.

When Corcoran returned he placed her phone on the table, saying that they retrieved it from Patrick's possessions. As he didn't say anything else about it, she was sure they had found nothing incriminating on it. He thanked her for her help and said that she was free to go. "No doubt," he added, "the British police will want to talk with you as well." Although his expression didn't change he seemed almost human. The flak he'd been expecting from the Bureau hadn't been too damaging. He didn't fully understand why, unless Dwyer's death was for some reason not as catastrophic to the Administration as he had imagined it would be. There was often an inside story that his clearance grade did not give him access to. At least Corcoran's job wasn't on the line but his pride was still hurt. Maybe he would recover and regroup; maybe he wouldn't.

Maura walked out on weak legs. It was a bright, cold day and the air was bracing. During the drive back to the hotel she didn't focus on anything in particular; her thoughts were mixed up and sporadic like the images in a dream. If there was a recurring theme it was her desire to go home as soon as possible.

All of the prize-winners and their minder, Art, had left the hotel, which seemed strange without them. She fetched her air ticket from her room and went downstairs to the lobby where a receptionist helped her re-book on the next available flight to Heathrow. There wasn't one until ten o'clock the next day.

She went back to her room and, with some trepidation, put in a call to Harold, but she only got the answering machine. The message was in his voice and she was startled to hear it. She wondered why he had put on the answering machine; it would only be about ten at night in England. Perhaps the neighbours and well-wishers were pestering him. He never did like answering the phone in the house, and sometimes compared its insistent ring to the shrill tantrums of an undisciplined child. She started to pack and was reminded of the start of her trip; it all seemed a very long time ago. She had a lonely evening ahead of her and a longer night. The ghost of Patrick was everywhere in the room, his voice, face and touch. She wondered if it was really over.

CHAPTER 21

OVER BREAKFAST STANLEY scanned the newspapers, including those from his own State. It was a habit he couldn't break even though his press officer produced a summary of all relevant items each and every day and emailed them to him.

"Strange how Dwyer's gone off the front pages already," he mused aloud. "Of course he always did prefer a low profile." He buttered a slice of toast and read on. Several liberal journalists were rabbiting on as usual about the cosy relationship between big business and the Administration while the more mainstream hacks deplored the weakness of the security arrangements.

Evelyn sat in silence, still shocked by the savage turn of events which had, in less than a second, deprived her of her dream. Stanley had, in a public statement, referred to his great sadness at the untimely death of his friend and colleague but he didn't mean a word of it. Lillian had expressed her condolences too, but she still couldn't understand how such a force of nature could be so suddenly and easily dispatched.

"Of course it must have been a dreadful shock for you," Stanley said, looking over his half-moon reading glasses.

Evelyn glanced at him but his face gave nothing away. She responded with a question, "Who do you think was responsible?"

"The agencies are following some leads," he said. "Probably the APF."

"But why?"

"Oh, some bizarre notion that Dwyer and Kaltronics were an evil influence on mankind. The world is full of craziness." He sighed and looked out at the morning mist that lay over Bethesda; it showed no sign of dispersing. "Well, Dwyer knew the risks. He wasn't an innocent abroad."

A cold shudder went through Evelyn. It was as if Stanley's callousness was designed to bait her. A crazy notion seized her; had Stanley deliberately absented himself from the Ball in the knowledge that something was going to happen? No, that was too much even for him. She would have to control these flights of fancy.

"You'll miss him," she said neutrally, meaning the funds he provided.

"He was part of the landscape." But, Stanley reflected, in the final analysis no more than that. He remembered that day in the garden when Dwyer lectured him about geopolitics as if he were telling him something he didn't already know, or something the CIA and FEMA had not already been crawling over for years. Dwyer wasn't even in the game and yet he had the arrogance to lecture a senior congressman. Stanley went back to the newspapers, going through them with great speed.

"What about your second term?" She was more than entitled to ask; it would affect her as much as him, perhaps more.

"Preparations are well in hand." He didn't elaborate but she was left with the distinct impression that he had found other backers. If so, that meant he had been putting out feelers for some time. Maybe Lawrence had not been as indispensable as he had thought. She had always known how calculating Stanley could be, but this surpassed everything, and it frightened her in a way.

"But you'll miss Lawrence's ... support?" she pressed.

"Not so as you'd notice." He looked up. "Perhaps not as much as you."

"What does that mean?"

"Did you enjoy your last night together?"

The blade struck home though she hardly felt it pierce the skin. "What?"

"Evelyn, Evelyn, don't kid a kidder. I know what went on. You're so obvious I can read you like a book."

His condescension infuriated her and goaded a reaction.

"You ... you spied on me?"

"Don't be so operatic. It was as plain as day." With calibrated movements he dropped a sugar cube into his second cup of coffee and stirred it slowly.

"And you don't care, do you?"

"Not much. You're not going to talk about it. And Dwyer can't. So," he spread his hands in a gesture of acceptance, "damage control all round."

She had an urge to shake him out of his maddening complacency. He seemed to be devoid of feeling. She wondered, not for the first time, if he was on medication. She watched him push the newspapers aside and go over the text of an introductory spiel he would give at a press briefing later on. He nodded his head intermittently as he read, as if it were a music score which needed the right tempo, intonation and phrasing. He was literally rehearsing for a performance, and it struck her that the part he played had taken him over completely.

Then out of the blue – and as if he had been harbouring similar thoughts about her – he said, "By the way your act never really impressed me."

"What act? What are you talking about?"

"You like playing romantic victims. It was a great scenario. Young sensitive girl loses boy next door. Never gets over it. Marries Dick Dastardly on the rebound. Becomes a celebrity but regards duties as a meaningless chore. Nothing can compensate for the pain in her heart. Eventually the boy next door becomes successful and returns. She now has it all. No trade-offs. She has her cake and eats it. But then fate slips the old lead ball into the musket and the boy next door gets himself shot. And the lady is distraught…" He gave her a big smile and continued, "…or is she? Maybe she has even better lines now. Maybe she becomes a truly great heroine…"

"You're mad!" She fought for control, to conceal how the taunts had found their mark. She was used to his indifference but this thinly veiled hatred was something new and disturbing. Long held suspicions coalesced in her mind and became a fact. "Do the voters know you're gay?" She could hardly believe that she'd said it. Now there was no way back.

"It took you a long time to figure that out," he said evenly.

"So, you don't …?" She was astounded by his calm reaction.

"Deny it?" He finished the sentence for her. "Of course not. Why should I? It's part of who I am."

"The election…"

"It's all a matter of discretion and I know I can count on yours." He turned a page of the speech and made a note in the margin.

"What makes you so sure?" Her voice was not as steady as she would have wished.

He removed the half-glasses and laid them on the table. "Because, my dear, you don't want to give anything up either." He carefully folded his napkin, laid it on the table and went out of the room.

He conferred with William and the press secretary and then the three men walked through a connecting corridor to the press room. It was a full house; virtually all of the national media were represented. The press secretary thanked them for coming and introduced Stanley, who walked to the podium, saluting many of the familiar faces in the audience. He presented his introductory statement which contained a glimpse of his vision of the future, namely a strong and prosperous America predicated on continuing dynamic leadership. Towards the end of the speech – in which he mentioned the work of CASA several times – he referred to the need to "put recent tragic events behind us and go forward with renewed confidence."

It was, however, the recent tragic events which were uppermost in the minds of the assembled journalists. Questions came thick and fast.

Stanley referred to an earlier statement he had made on the assassination and added, "The tragic occurrence is under active investigation. It would not be appropriate for me to say more at this point in time." He acknowledged another hand that shot up.

"It's rumoured that the APF were responsible. Could you comment on that?"

"It is too early to say. There are several radical groups which would bear scrutiny. For all we know at this stage it could have been a personal matter..."

"A vendetta?"

"We just don't know yet. All avenues are being pursued, including of course the lapse in security arrangements."

Several journalists followed up on the security angle and Stanley fielded their questions with aplomb. Lillian, who had arrived late and was seated towards the back of the room, entered the fray.

"Isn't it true that Lawrence Dwyer was close to you and supported your electoral campaigns?"

"I knew him fairly well, yes. We come from the same state. And it is true that he helped the party with his time and energy. As did many others, I might add. We will miss him a great deal." As he bowed his head several videocams at the back of the hall zoomed in for close-ups.

"He also contributed money, substantial funds," Lillian persisted.

"There were some party contributions, I believe," Stanley said. "That is part of our system, Ms. Bartok. If people wish to make donations that is their right."

"But Kaltronics is a major arms manufacturer. They have affiliate companies here in Washington. Are you saying that no military contracts were ever put his way by your committee?" Lillian wasn't at all sure she would have much success with this line of questioning. But at least she had the satisfaction of noticing that her peers were not interrupting her. They had tacitly given her the floor. She was also aware that she might be making life a little more difficult for Evelyn. Still, she was a big girl now who could quite obviously take care of herself.

"This Administration does not engage in favouritism, Ms. Bartok. Nor does CASA. Mr. Dwyer knew that and accepted it. The procedures for tendering are rigorous and transparent. Only competitive bids are considered. These self-imposed rules are strictly enforced. If anyone in this room knows of even one instance where standards have slipped I for one would be grateful to be informed of it." He looked around the room as if challenging someone to come up with an example. No-one did.

Lillian had one more shot in her locker. "Is it not true that Kaltronics is developing a radically new weapons system that will…"

"Sorry to interrupt, Ms Bartok, but I have no knowledge of that, and for me to speculate would be wrong, misleading and quite possibly damaging to national security."

Lillian held her peace; she needed more evidence. Stanley was becoming frighteningly good at this. He could afford to hold the high moral ground because all such deals were so secret that only the principals knew about them and they weren't going to talk. They had it all sewn up; there was no way in.

The questioning turned to the economy and the budget deficit. Stanley acquitted himself well. A young Turk from The Post took up the running. He argued that the Administration could only square the circle if the economy began to perform exceptionally well and continued to do so. Stanley nodded. He had no argument with that and used the opportunity to stress the need for a continuation of strong leadership. The latter spawned a few questions about a second term and Stanley let it be known that he was keen to finish the programme he had started, assuming that the people wanted to see it to completion. After that digression the correspondent from The Post returned to his theme.

"Where," he asked, "are the resources to come from? Economic miracles don't just happen. Have we discovered vast quantities of oil or other valuable resources?"

"There's no miracle involved," Stanley said with a smile. "But it has always seemed to me that we have not fully exploited those advantages which we already have. I'm talking about America's leadership in the area of information technology. What we are working towards is a strategy which combines technology with the newly emerging geo-political and trading scenes." He smiled plausibly. "I know this all sounds a little vague and general, but the strategy will work. Trust me. I am prepared to stake my political future on it."

Other journalists rowed in with questions about the risks of depending on foreign markets and the need for greater productivity at home. But Lillian had heard enough. Information technology was code for hyper-smart weapons, and the trading scene meant exporting them to countries that would soon be in thrall to America. It was obvious that he had other arms manufacturers lined up to take the place of Kaltronics. Dwyer's death had only put the slightest dent in the grand plan. Some strategy.

And from his point of view it would work; that was why he had been so confident. To start the ball rolling, CASA would dip into the aid budget and the social spend. Then the gratitude of the arms industry would make him impregnable. The next stage would be to extract resources from newly colonised countries in the same way as former empires had done. It was a virtuous circle: subsidies, arms, domination, free resources, more subsidies, more arms, etc., etc. Indeed, Stanley was so self-assured that it was impossible to needle him into a rash statement. Lillian gave up on the briefing and slipped out.

Later that afternoon she tried calling Evelyn

from her office. She tried again from her apartment at about eight p.m. Still no answer. She had the strongest impression that Evelyn had finally made a choice, or rather that Lawrence's death had made the choice for her. In any event the ranks had closed.

She went into the kitchen to start the pasta. She wasn't sure if Boyd would be joining her or not but, to be on the safe side, she decided to cook for two. It was only when the pan was coming to the boil that she saw his note. He had to go circuit-training in the gym and would probably spend the night on campus. She thought this was lame, and wondered if it didn't mean the beginning of the end.

CHAPTER 22

FROM LA GUARDIA, Maura had to take a cab to Kennedy and that meant retracing some of the steps she'd taken with Patrick in New York. The images that came into her head were too fresh and painful to be memories and yet that is what they were. He was dead; somehow she would have to accept that fact.

She felt desperately lonely as the aircraft rose above the clouds and nosed out over the Atlantic. The cumulative effects of the last ten days took their toll and she fell, mercifully, into a deep sleep. When dinner was being served a stewardess tried gently to wake her and decided to leave her be.

When she got through customs at Heathrow there was the usual crowd pressing forward at the arrivals to greet incoming passengers. Suddenly she saw Harold. He came forward and embraced her, patting her on the back as she started to cry. Part of the crowd stirred and came alive; the tabloids were out in force. Fortunately, two detective inspectors from Scotland Yard helped her through as questions were hurled aggressively at her.

As she got out of range she thought she heard a journalist ask about her relationship with the assassin. But maybe it was her imagination. At one point she stumbled, having been temporarily blinded by the cameras flashes.

Harold held her elbow. "You have Barbara Woodside to thank for this," he said grimly.

She was led to an unmarked police car. It – and the one following – took off at speed.

"It's good … to be back," she stammered. "Are you all right, Harold?"

"I'm OK… You?"

"Yes." It was difficult to say more with the two detectives in the front of the car.

"I apologise for this, Mrs. Crowther," one of them said. "But we need a debriefing. Do you feel up to it now or should we take you home first?"

She looked at Harold. "Now," she said.

"Very good. I promise you it won't take long."

She was brought to a Commander's office in the main Scotland Yard building. He and one of the Inspectors sat across from her at a leather-topped conference table. Harold had been asked to wait outside; it was a matter of procedure.

Although they went over much the same ground as Corcoran, the interview was less intimidating. They spent more time on the events which had occurred in England and they were obviously cross-checking her version against that already given by Harold. It was pointed out to her, albeit in a polite way, that she should have gone to the police despite her fears for her husband. She had the vaguest impression that they had been embarrassed by the US authorities. Her real fear was that they would investigate her relationship with Patrick but, in the event, they hardly touched on that, except in a very general way. At the end of the interview the commander thanked her and wished her well. He walked her to the lift, where Harold was waiting. They declined the offer of a police car and took a minicab home.

Crossing her own threshold was almost a rite of passage; a chapter of her life had closed. She took in all of the familiar objects, the coats on the hall stand, the floral wallpaper that she'd never got around to changing, the mahogany telephone seat that needed re-polishing.

"It's over," she said. "I can't believe it's over."

"Me neither," Harold said.

She left her bags in the hall and they went through to the kitchen where Harold put the kettle on.

"I asked the neighbours to respect our privacy," he said.

"That was considerate." She opened a kitchen press and got a couple of aspirin which she swallowed with a glass of water.

"Are you sure you're all right?"

"Just a headache." She sat weakly at the table. What was wrong with her? She should at least have been relieved but she never felt emptier. "It must've been very hard on you."

"I thought every second would be my last. They were nasty bits of work I can tell you." He poured out the tea and set a plate of biscuits on the table.

"How many were there?"

"At least three," he said. "But probably more. I couldn't be sure. They kept me in a dark, filthy cellar and they wore balaclavas all the time. Bastards!" He thought of the degradation of his first day of freedom and could still smell the pig-swill. He had also lodged a formal complaint about the sergeant in Saffron Walden and hoped he would be sacked.

"Have you had a medical check-up?"

He nodded. "I'm OK. On the surface at least. There are bound to be psychological scars. Even the strongest constitution can't come through that kind of experience unscathed." He helped himself to a biscuit and passed the plate to her.

"Did they … mistreat you?"

"They didn't cut off any fingers if that's what you mean. But they knew how to punish in subtler ways." He poured himself a whiskey and offered her one. She declined, feeling numb enough already.

"You've lost weight," she observed. "Have you had a decent meal since you … came home?" She got up and looked in the fridge; there was precious little there. She was about to go out to the garage to check the deep freeze but he said he couldn't eat anyway.

"We could order a take-away," she suggested. "It's probably not too late."

"I'm fine, honestly. Unless you want something?"

"No." She had a sudden urge for a cigarette but she had quit eight years ago at his instigation and it would be downright stupid to start again.

"Let's go to bed," he suggested.

"I wonder if the sheets are aired?"

He went upstairs to switch on the electric blanket. Then he came down to fetch the bags she'd left in the hall. She finished her tea and put the things in the dishwasher. When she went upstairs he was already in bed, reading. She brushed her teeth in the en suite bathroom and changed into her nightdress. When she got into bed he turned towards her.

"I missed you," he said in a thick voice.

"Oh, Harold. I don't think … I'm whacked out. Do you mind if …?"

"No." He turned on his light and picked up the Financial Times.

Maura lay awake for a long time after he'd fallen asleep. She felt trapped in the Laura Ashley bedroom. The curtains matched the wallpaper – all those similar flowers and buds; everything matched. It was suffocating. She wanted to kick off the bedclothes and the electric blanket and run down the street, breathing in the night air. She got out of bed – carefully so as not to disturb him – and went downstairs, took another couple of aspirin and sat in the kitchen, holding her head.

Harold went to work the next day and she mooned around the house almost afraid to go out. She didn't want to meet anyone, least of all Barbara Woodside. The New Year was well under way and nothing was different; there had been no turning point – just the same number of hours to get through in a day. But she must have changed because she had never experienced such weariness before.

During the weeks following Harold put her under some pressure to resume her work in the surgery. She forced herself to go in about every second day to keep the books in order. She noticed the first signs of spring in the garden and, with an effort of will, made a start on a long-deferred project of transplanting some shrubs in the hope of making a little rock garden. She had gradually renewed old acquaintances, including Barbara, who apologised profusely for blurting out the news of Harold's 'escape' to a reporter. Maura had even gone back to her bridge club. Everything had returned to normal with one exception; herself. She was simply going through the motions. Barbara sensed this and suggested a holiday in the sun.

"It would do you a power of good," she said. "After all you've been through."

Maura reflected on the idea but she was just too listless and couldn't summon the effort of trying to convince Harold, who was now back in his comfortable routine. He and his partner had brought a young dentist into the practice; this allowed Harold a little more time for golf and for his investments. Apart from an occasional nightmare and the odd verbal attack on his abductors, he had put the matter behind him.

"Life goes on," was his only advice to Maura. She didn't belittle this advice; she just couldn't put it into practice. Conjugal relations of a sort had been restored. The act itself meant little to her but he seemed content; if he detected any remoteness on her part he didn't say anything.

She tried not to think about Patrick but his image lurked in her mind. He had changed her life and now that he was gone it seemed empty of meaning. The Sky news bulletins which covered US foreign policy suggested that Patrick's view of American hegemony had been right all along, except in one particular: the wheels turned even without Lawrence Dwyer. So Patrick's sacrifice – that was how she now saw it – was for nothing. Other powerful, unelected people had apparently sprung up to fill the vacuum.

One evening Harold put down his paper to ask how she'd spent her day. Her reply was as vague as her day had been.

"You'd think you'd have pulled yourself together by now," he remarked.

"I'm all right."

"I doubt it. You'd almost think that you got the worst of it…"

"How do you mean?" She used the remote control to turn down the volume on the TV.

"I was the one who was kidnapped at gunpoint and tied up in a stinking hole for two weeks." He had never mentioned the bucket or the fact that he had intended going back to the cellar during those first hours of panic-filled freedom before the tractor came along. Indeed he tried hard to obliterate those symbols of degradation from his mind.

"It was no picnic for me," she replied, though her heart wasn't in it.

"Well, I mean, you went off tripping around the States…"

"To save your life," she said a little more heatedly. She should have realised even then that he was too strait-laced to be murdered; he would go on to old age and die in his bed, chewing mints to sweeten his breath, maybe even flossing his teeth.

"You'd have gone anyway."

"I don't follow…"

He took off his glasses and wiped the lenses with a strip of chamois. "You had the insane notion all along. You were hell-bent on it. Oh yes, you'd have gone. On your own if you had to."

"You refused to come." Why go on with this wrangling, she thought. Just let it be. But she sensed there was a buried agenda which needed to be brought to the surface.

"Because I told you not to go on that damn quiz show. I told you. You can't deny that."

"And I disobeyed you?"

"Yes." He ignored or failed to recognise her sarcasm.

So she made it more explicit. "My Lord and Master." She wanted to turn up the volume on the TV; Coronation Street was worth more than this harangue.

"You know I was right all along. None of this would have happened if you'd listened to me."

"That wasn't your reason then." She was being drawn into this against her will. How could he be so wrong-headed and self-righteous at the same time?

"Nevertheless," he said heavily, "you caused a great deal of trouble. A great deal."

Suddenly she banged her fists against the arm of the sofa. "It happened because it fucking well happened."

He was on his feet, flushed; she had never spoken to him like that before. She thought he was going to strike her; she might even have welcomed it. "You're not well," he said finally. "You should see a psychiatrist. You've been moping around for weeks now. Get yourself sorted out."

"Don't tell me what to do!" She stood and confronted him.

"What the hell got into you over there?"

"Maybe I learnt how to stand up for myself, how to manage in impossible situations without anyone breathing down my neck."

"Well, you're back here now. And I expect you to conduct yourself in a more appropriate manner."

"That's not going to happen. I will not conform to your pathetic little world. And if you don't accept me as I am, then we should go our separate ways."

His eyes bulged behind the glasses but his voice was less angry and held a conciliatory note. "You don't mean that."

"I do, Harold. I've never been more serious in my life. You're going to have to change. Otherwise I don't see a future for us."

"Don't be…" His voice tailed off.

She felt there was a chance that her words found their mark. As he left the room to go upstairs, he turned and said, "I hope you feel better soon." It sounded like a genuine hope and not an instruction.

A couple of days later she went to her GP, Dr. Chalmers, who welcomed her into his untidy surgery.

"Well, the s/hero returns," he boomed. "You're one tough woman to have survived all those dangerous shenanigans. How in god's name are you, Maura?"

"You're supposed to tell me." His jovial manner was a tonic in itself and she found herself telling him a lot about her recent experiences – more than she had told Harold.

His mobile face registered surprise, sympathy and incredulity as she spoke. He looked at her closely, believing that the appearance of the face was one of the best aids to diagnosis. She found it a little disconcerting.

"You're looking well in spite of everything," he said. But Maura knew that he normally said 'looking great', so that meant she wasn't quite up to par. She told him how listless she felt, how she was just about coping, doing things by rote.

"It's probably a reaction to what you've been through," he said. "Believe it or not, there can often be a feeling of anti-climax even after nerve-racking experiences."

"But Harold isn't going through this and he bore the brunt of it." She felt a little guilty about concealing her affair with Patrick.

"Oh, Harold." Chalmers grinned. "He has his work and his golf. The only thing he worries about is his dignity."

True enough, she thought, but since the row about their future together, she thought he was making an effort. "I'm probably just run down."

"Well, let's have a look at you." He took her

vital signs and listened to her heart and lungs. He asked her to make a fist while he drew some blood.

"Now," he said, straightening up, "You can leave a sample of urine with the nurse and come back to me in two days and we'll see what the score is. But don't worry about it. And tell that husband of yours to whisk you off to the Bahamas."

When she returned the following Wednesday he did another test there and then. He turned his back on her while he washed his hands in the sink; then he sat behind his desk and looked across at her.

"You're not even rundown," he said. "You're pregnant."

At first it didn't register with her. But she saw that he was grinning from ear to ear.

"You're pregnant," he repeated. "As in, being with child."

"I don't ... believe it..."

"You'd better believe it. You are unquestionably in the family way."

"How ... long?" she asked breathlessly.

"Five or six weeks."

"Oh god." She didn't know whether to laugh or cry.

"Exactly." He gave her a conspiratorial look. "It must've been a fairly good vacation in the old US of A despite everything. Since I assume you weren't party to the kidnapping, I presume we're talking about an extreme version of the Stockholm syndrome…"

"Oh shit." She started to laugh. "After all this time … a child … It's incredible…" Her brow suddenly furrowed. What would Harold's reaction be? The fact that this thought came into her mind made her feel as if she were slipping back into a rut. She resolved there and then that if Harold proved to be a problem she would leave him. "I'll have to tell Harold, of course."

"It's not really for me to offer different advice, Maura." He didn't wear his professional manner very well. He looked at the ceiling for a while, then at the traffic visible from the main window of his surgery, then across the desk at her. "But does Harold…em… really have to know? I mean, you've…had relations with him since you came back?"

She nodded.

"Well, there's only a week or two in it at most. "That's well within the margin of … uncertainty, if I may call it that."

"But he may suspect deep down that … his sperm count is low." A child, she thought, god almighty.

"Harold?" Chalmers gave vent to the laughter he'd been bottling up. "He wouldn't think that in a million years. Never underestimate the male ego." He pulled out a handkerchief, blew his nose and wiped his eyes.

"But it wouldn't be fair to him," Maura said in a fairly token way.

"I can't advise you on moral grounds." Chalmers tried to recapture his formal manner. "But I know how much you both wanted a child, you especially. And Harold will love it to bits … A child will be good for you both. You can bring it with you to the practice, assuming you still want to do your job. Think of the alternatives."

"I have done." She also thought of the passport photo, the broad similarity of appearance. Wherever Patrick was now she had the impression that he would be smiling just as she was. Maybe he had failed to change the world but what he had given her was worth more than that as far as she was concerned. The world could look after itself. Life could be extraordinary. A child! Her heart soared.

She had decided before she even left the surgery. Chalmers was right, absolutely right. Poor Harold would be over the moon, boasting about his sprog on the nineteenth hole. Well, he deserved that. She felt more fondly disposed towards him than she had in a long while.

During the train journey home she watched a group of commuters strap-hanging, rolling with each jolt of the carriage. Poor sods, she thought, going about their boring business. They didn't have a gift from god like she had; she could hardly contain herself. Even the seedy back yards and grim out-houses that abutted the train-track would look fascinating to a toddler's eyes. Patrick or Patricia. The child would be loved, was already loved.

She thought of the strange impulse that had driven her to the quiz show and the bizarre events that followed. It was never just about seeing in the New Year, but rather about newness itself, the possibility of meaning other than good dentition. She had always sensed that there had to be more, and she was right.